THE CRYPTID CLUB

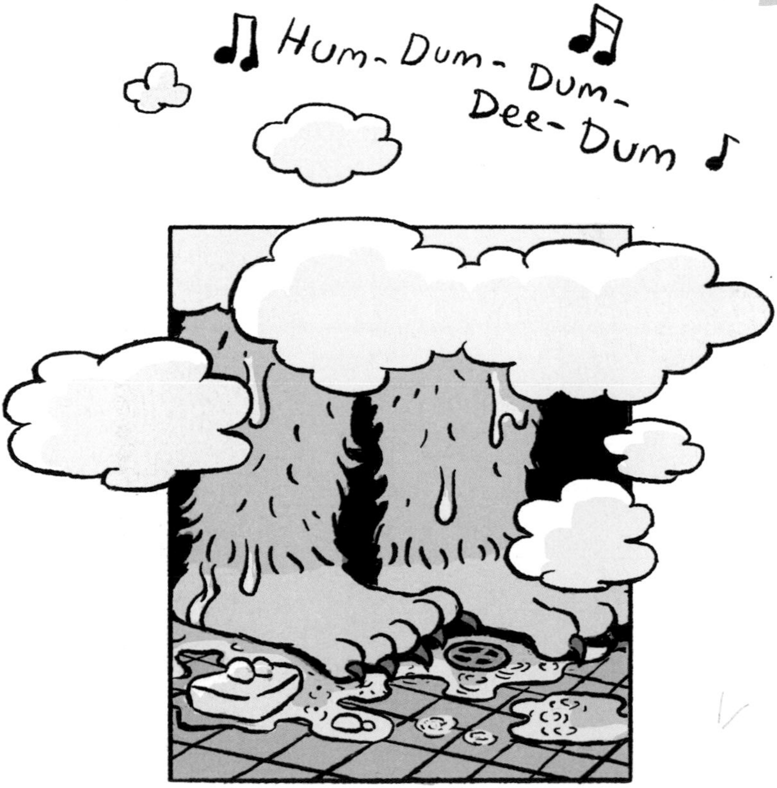
Hum-Dum-Dum-Dee-Dum

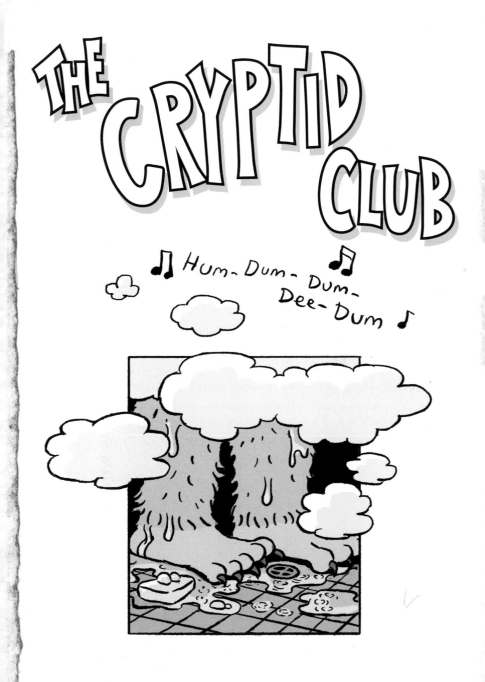

THE CRY

HarperAlley is an imprint of HarperCollins Publishers.

Cryptid Club #1: Bigfoot Takes the Field
Text copyright © 2022 by Michael Brumm
Illustrations copyright © 2022 by Jeff Mack
All rights reserved. Manufactured in Italy.
No part of this book may be used or reproduced in any manner whatsoever without written permission
except in the case of brief quotations embodied in critical articles and reviews. For information address
HarperCollins Children's Books, a division of HarperCollins Publishers,
195 Broadway, New York, NY 10007.
www.harperalley.com

Library of Congress Control Number: 2021933200
ISBN 978-0-06-306079-1 — ISBN 978-0-06-306078-4 (pbk.)

Typography by Joe Merkel
22 23 24 25 26   RTLO   10 9 8 7 6 5 4 3 2 1
❖
First Edition

PTID CLUB

CLUB

BIGFOOT TAKES THE FIELD

HARPER alley

An Imprint of HarperCollinsPublishers

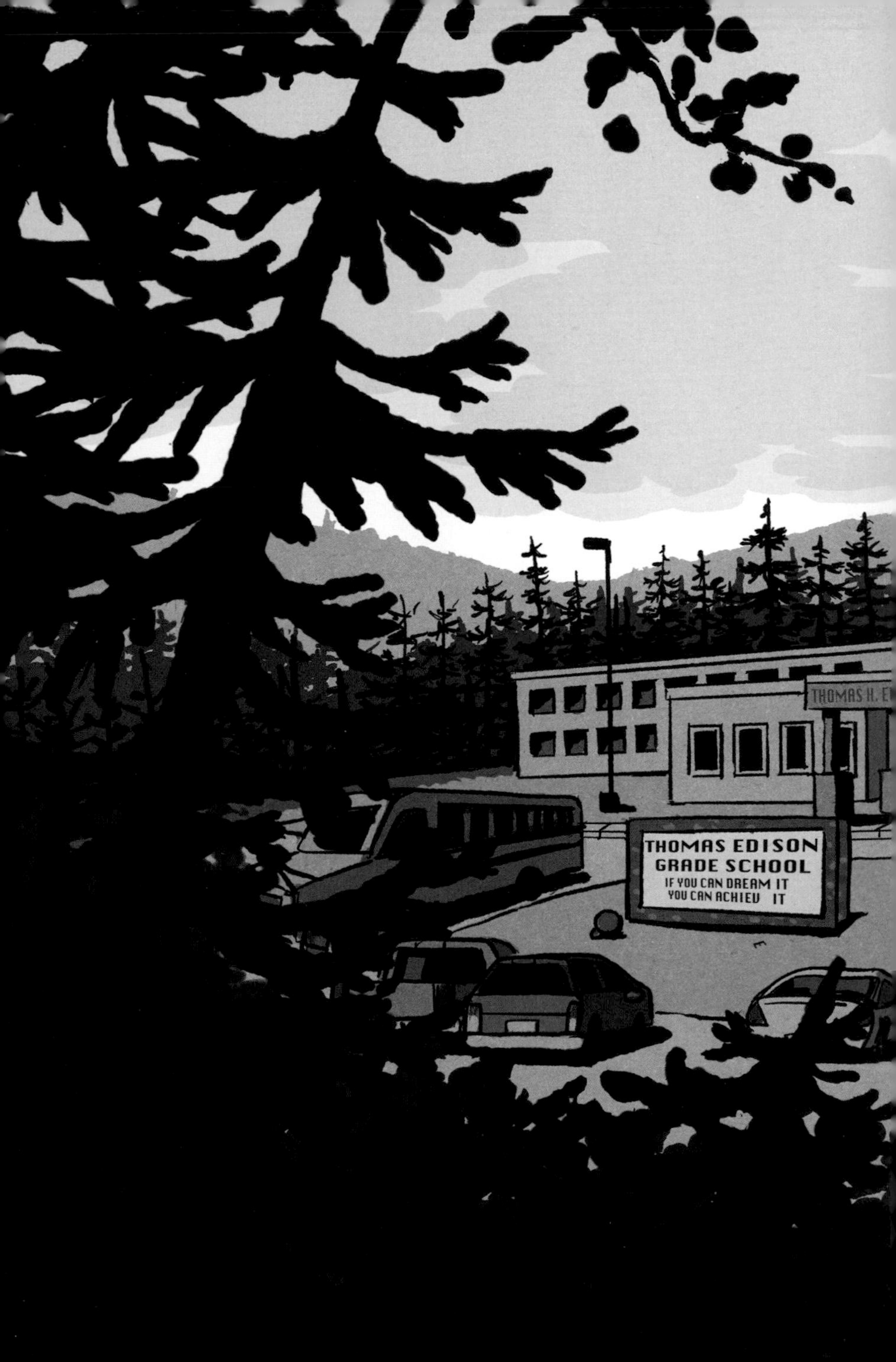
THOMAS H. E
THOMAS EDISON
GRADE SCHOOL
IF YOU CAN DREAM IT
YOU CAN ACHIEV IT

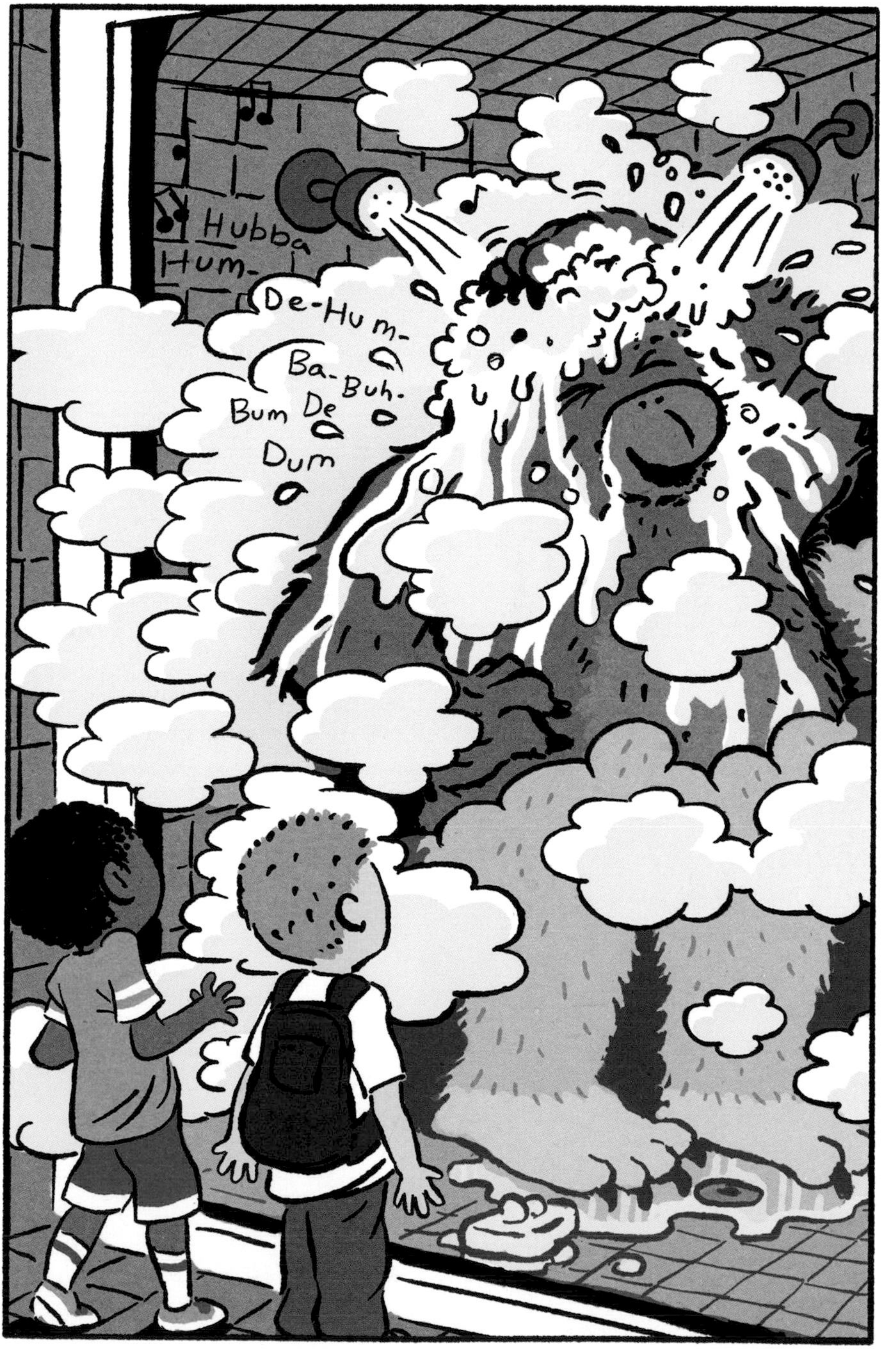
Hubba
Hum-
De-Hum-
Ba-Buh-
Bum De
Dum

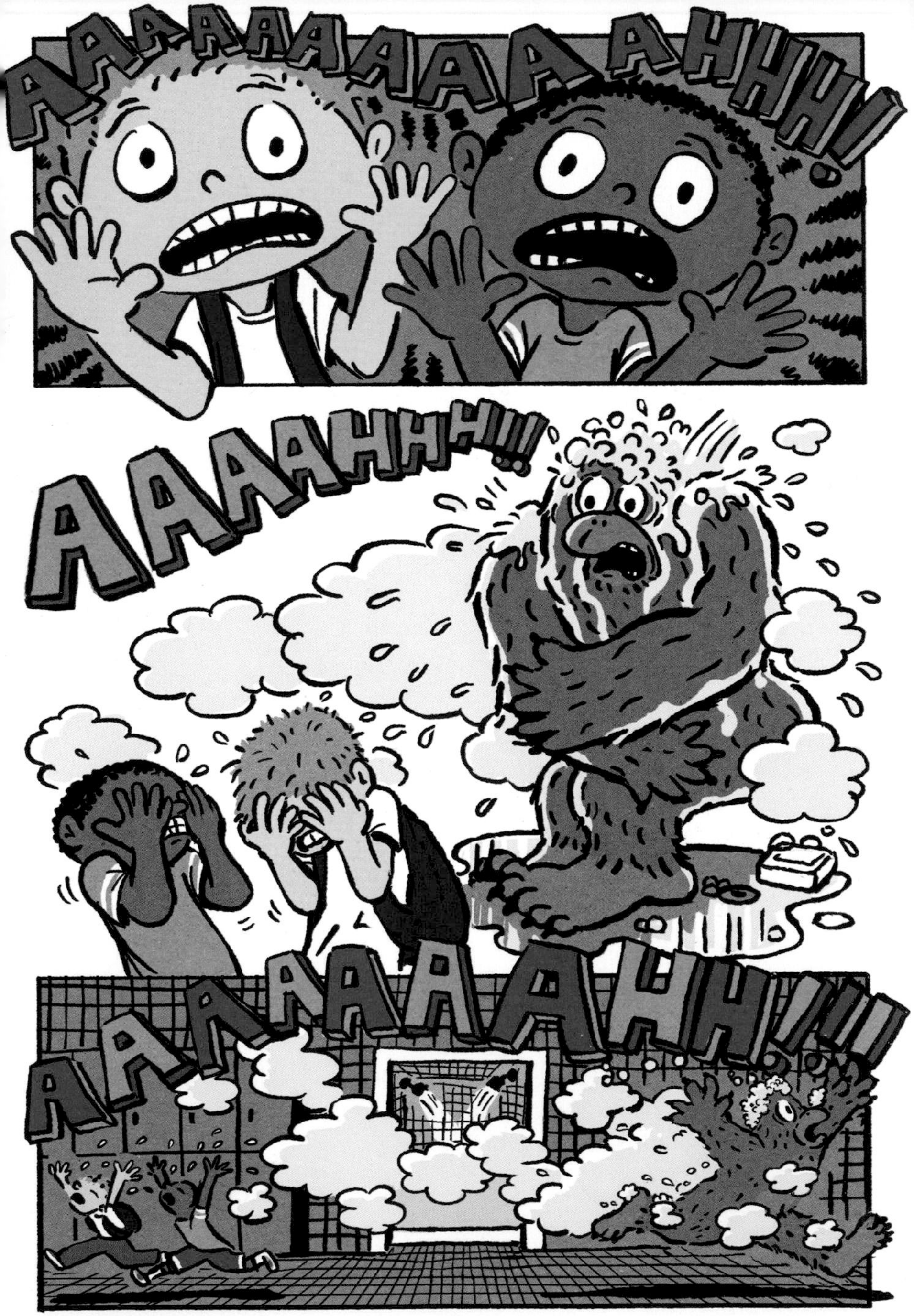
AAAAAAAAAAHHH!
AAAAHHH!!!
AAAAAAAAAHHH!!!!

9

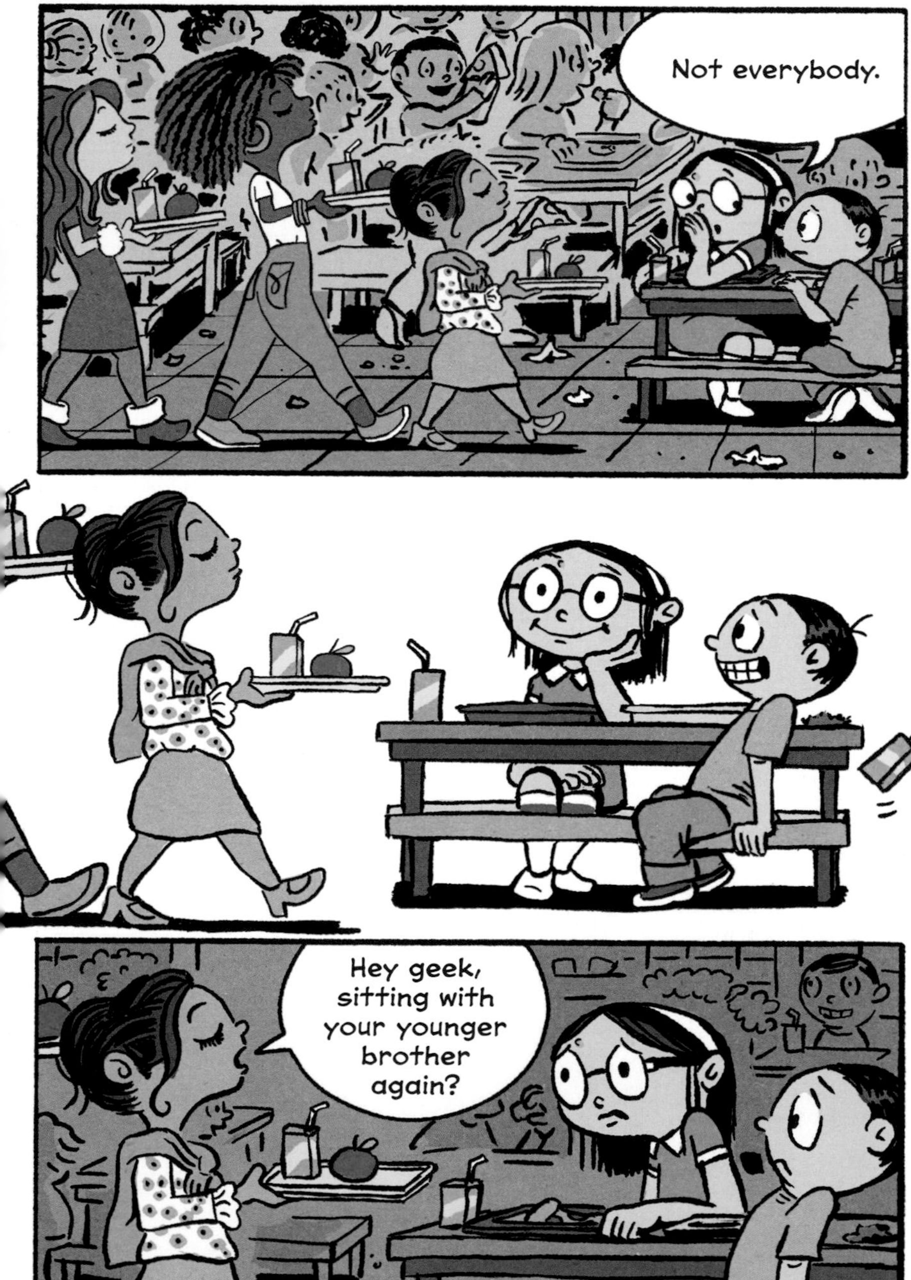
Not everybody.
Hey geek, sitting with your younger brother again?

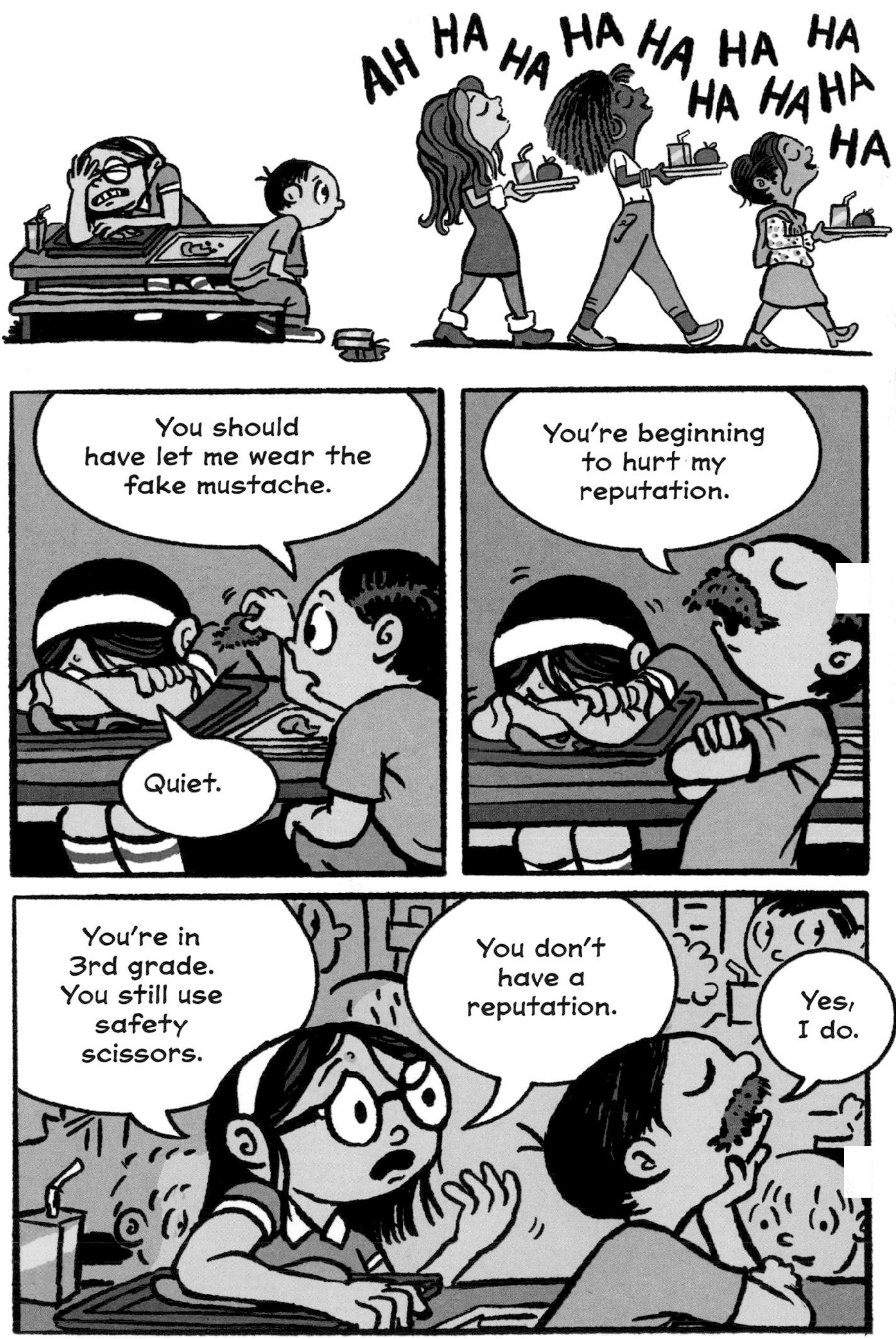
AH HA HA HA HA HA HA HA HA HA HA
You should have let me wear the fake mustache.
Quiet.
You're beginning to hurt my reputation.
You're in 3rd grade. You still use safety scissors.
You don't have a reputation.
Yes, I do.

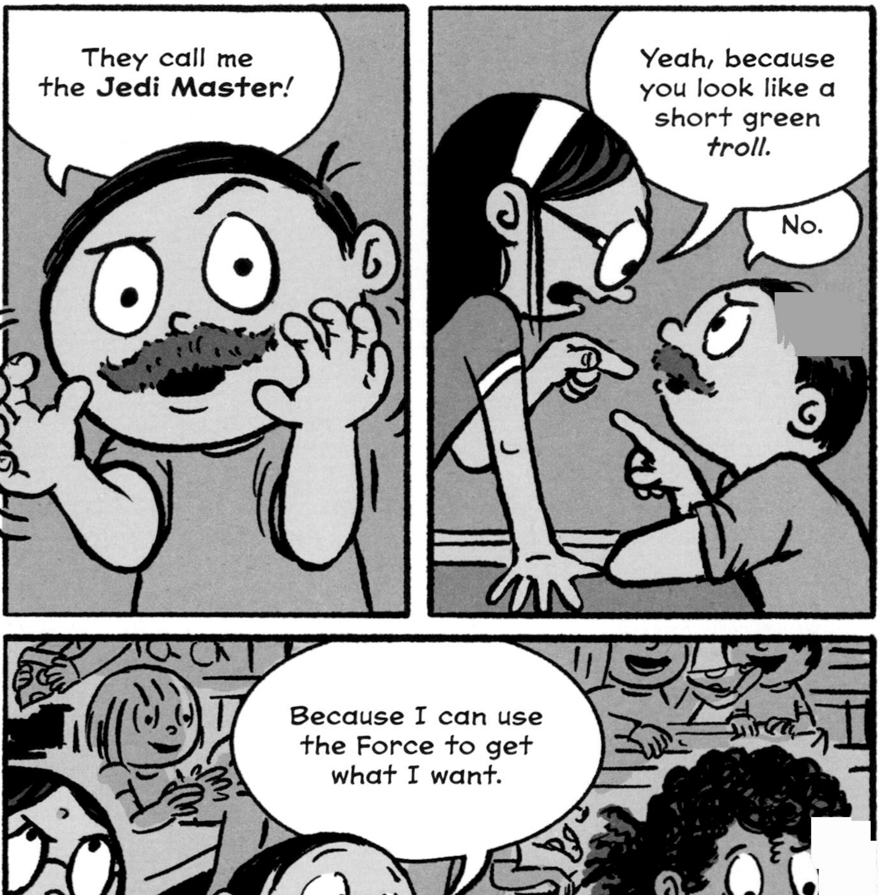
They call me the **Jedi Master**!
Yeah, because you look like a short green *troll.*
No.
Because I can use the Force to get what I want.

15

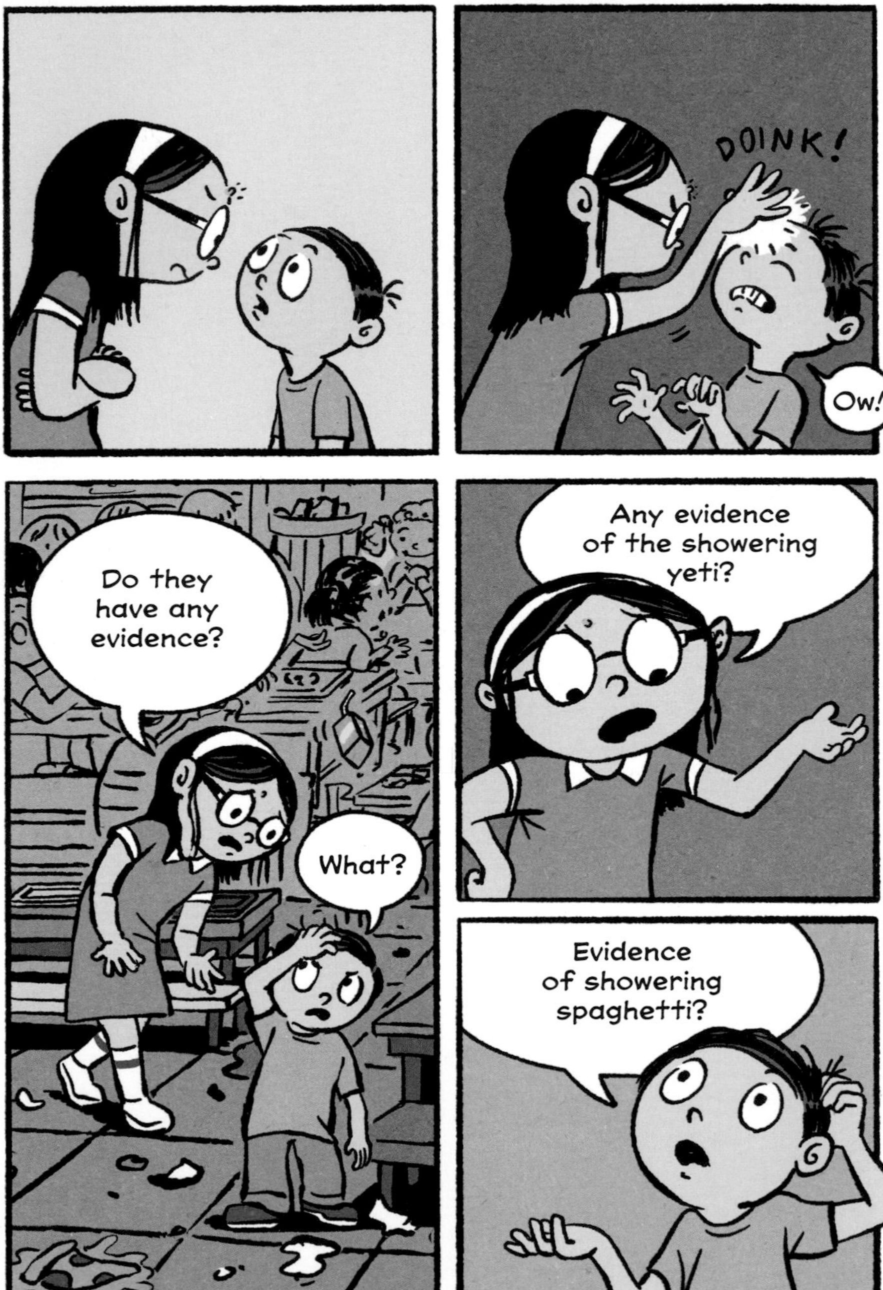
DOINK!
Ow!
Do they have any evidence?
What?
Any evidence of the showering yeti?
Evidence of showering spaghetti?

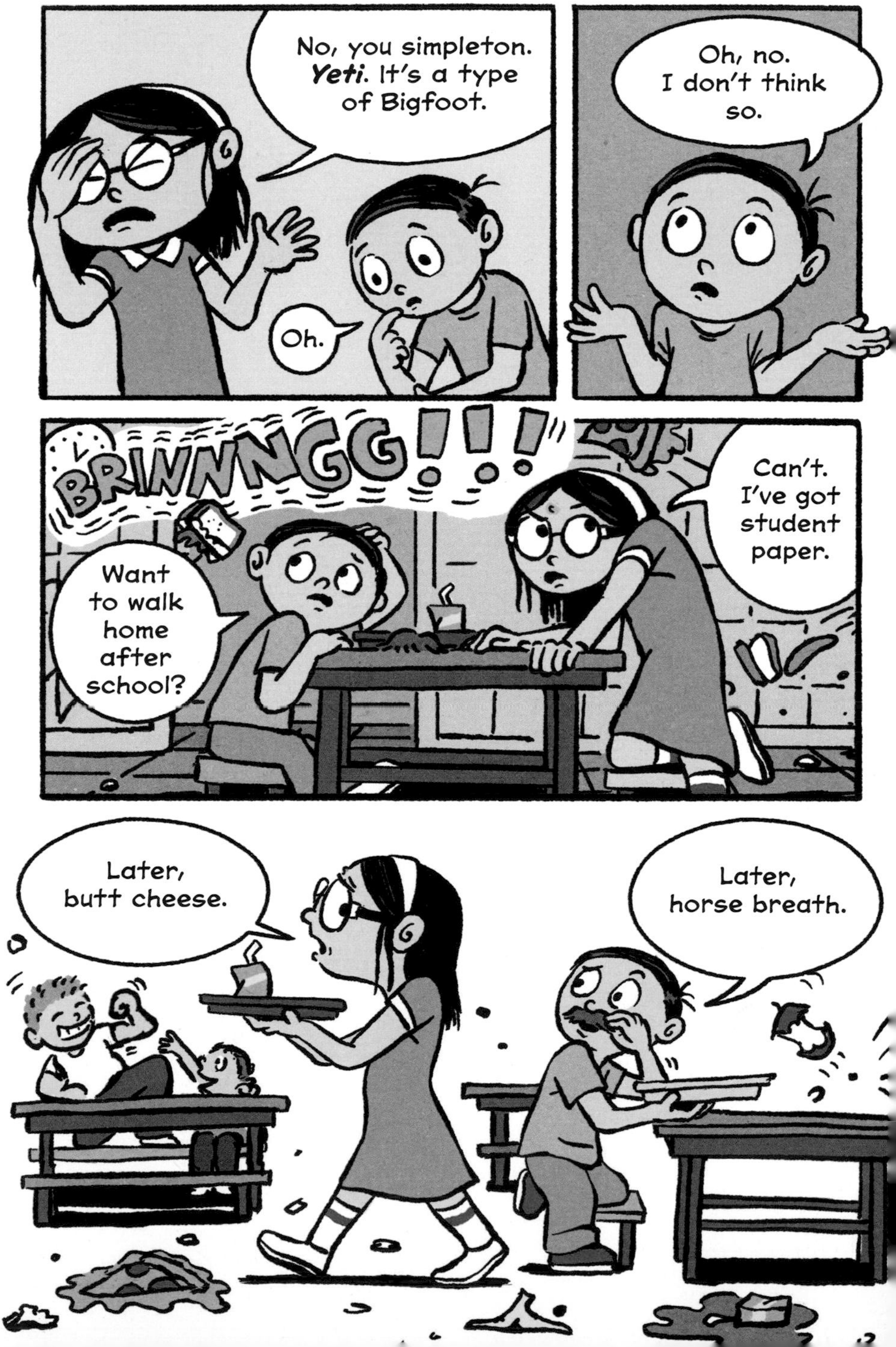
No, you simpleton. *Yeti*. It's a type of Bigfoot.
Oh.
Oh, no. I don't think so.
BRINNNGG!!!
Want to walk home after school?
Can't. I've got student paper.
Later, butt cheese.
Later, horse breath.

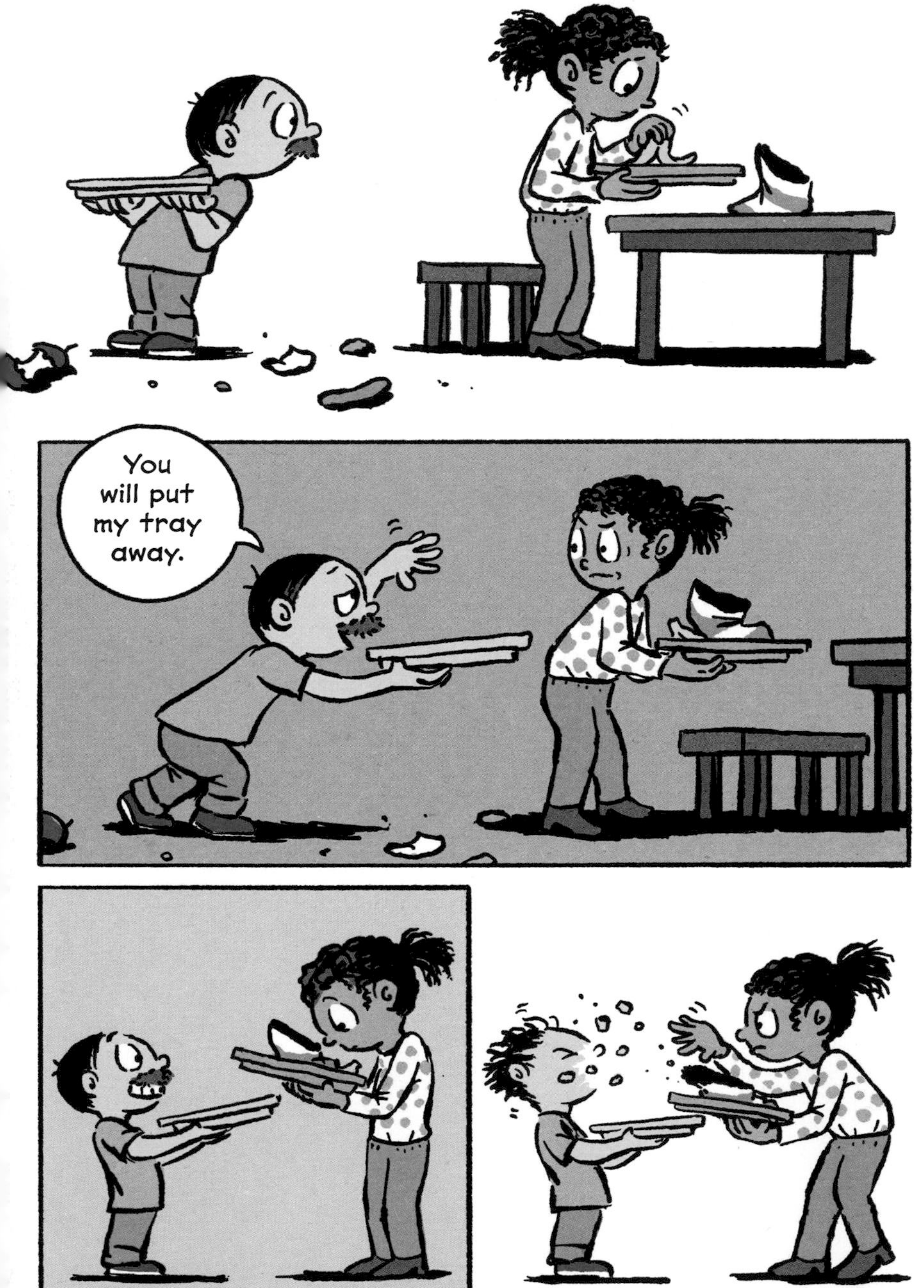
You will put my tray away.

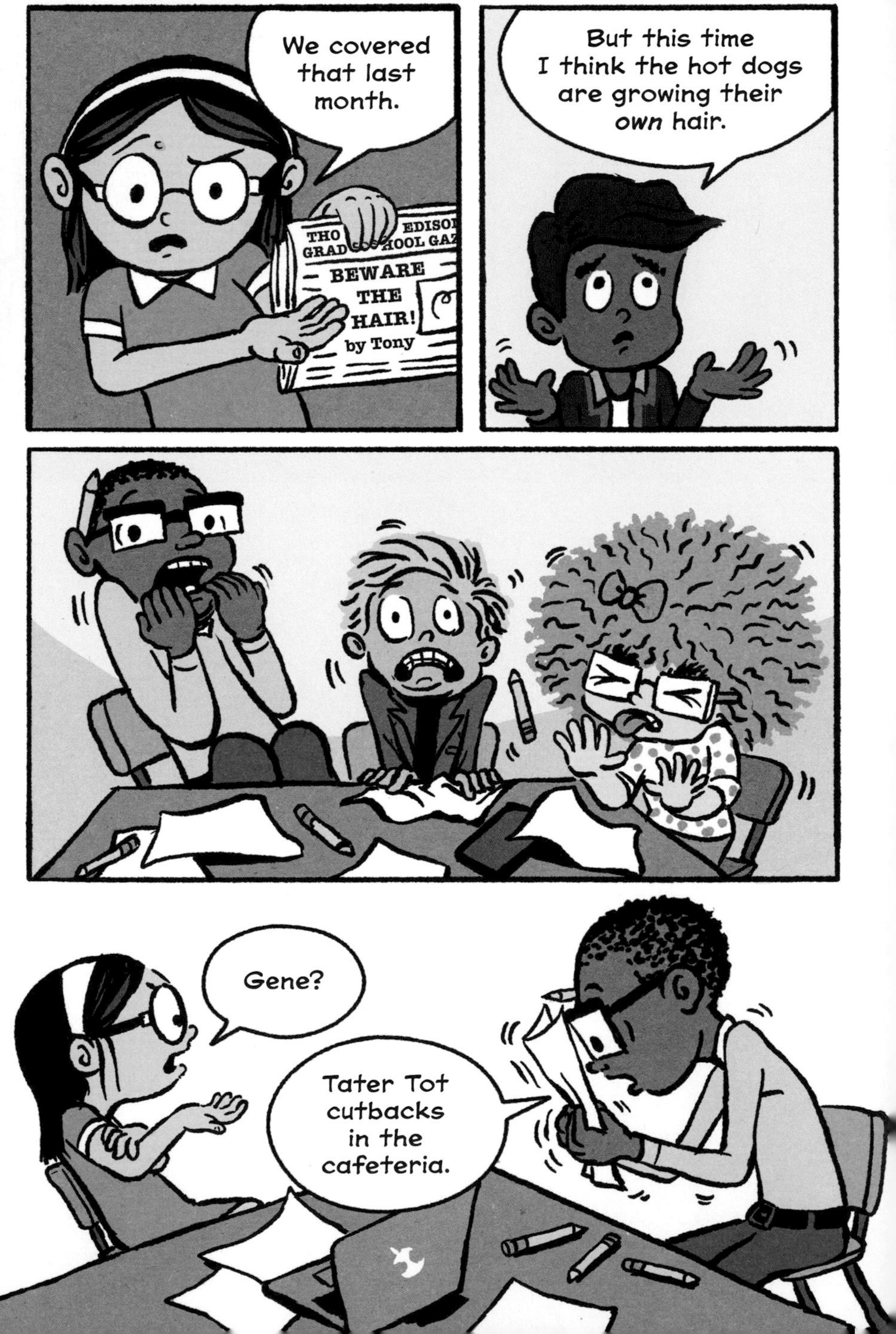
We covered that last month.
THO EDISO GRAD HOOL GAZ
BEWARE THE HAIR!
by Tony
But this time I think the hot dogs are growing their *own* hair.
Gene?
Tater Tot cutbacks in the cafeteria.

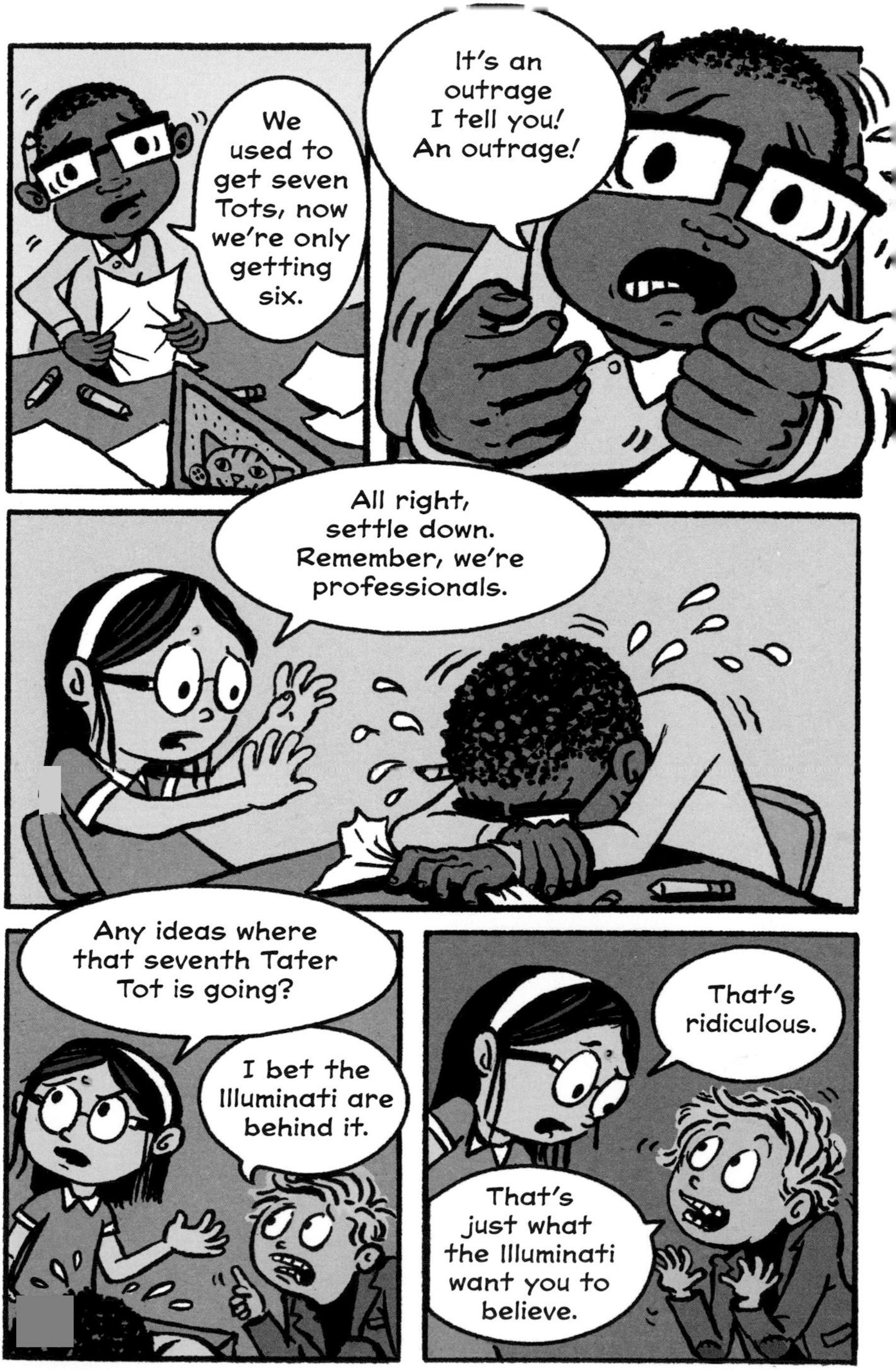
We used to get seven Tots, now we're only getting six.
It's an outrage I tell you! An outrage!
All right, settle down. Remember, we're professionals.
Any ideas where that seventh Tater Tot is going?
I bet the Illuminati are behind it.
That's ridiculous.
That's just what the Illuminati want you to believe.

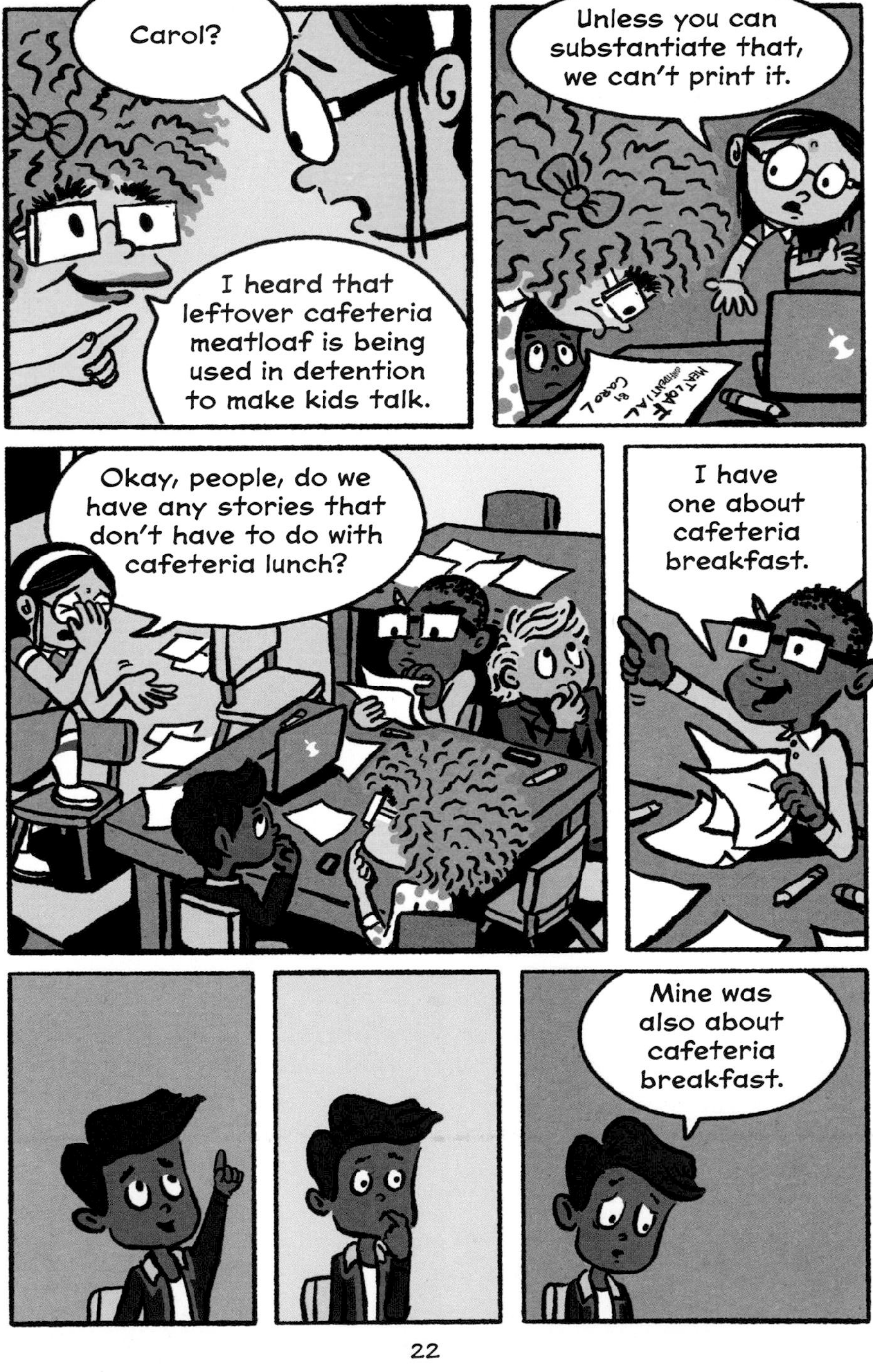
Carol?
I heard that leftover cafeteria meatloaf is being used in detention to make kids talk.
Unless you can substantiate that, we can't print it.
Okay, people, do we have any stories that don't have to do with cafeteria lunch?
I have one about cafeteria breakfast.
Mine was also about cafeteria breakfast.

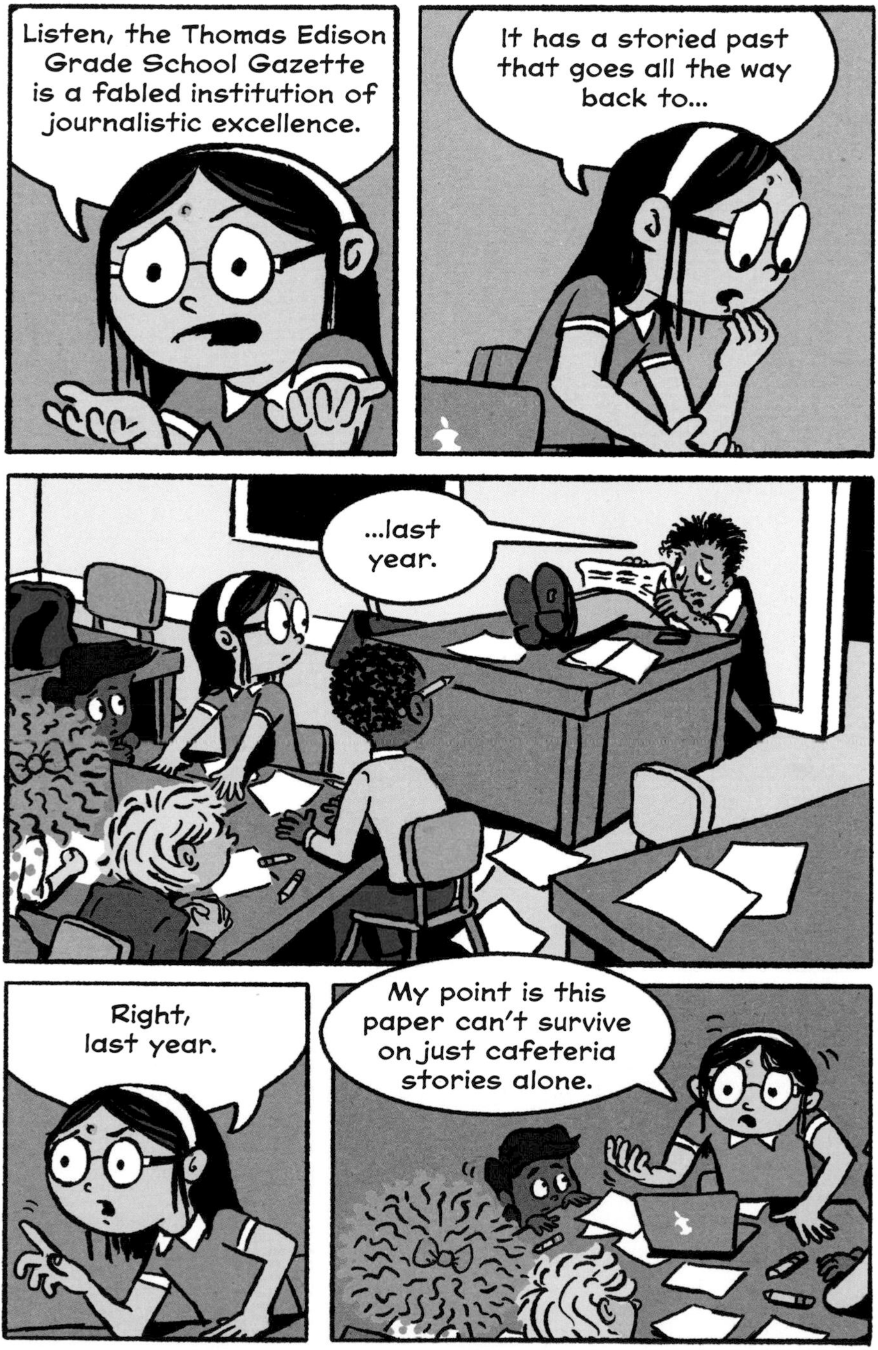
Listen, the Thomas Edison Grade School Gazette is a fabled institution of journalistic excellence.
It has a storied past that goes all the way back to...
...last year.
Right, last year.
My point is this paper can't survive on just cafeteria stories alone.

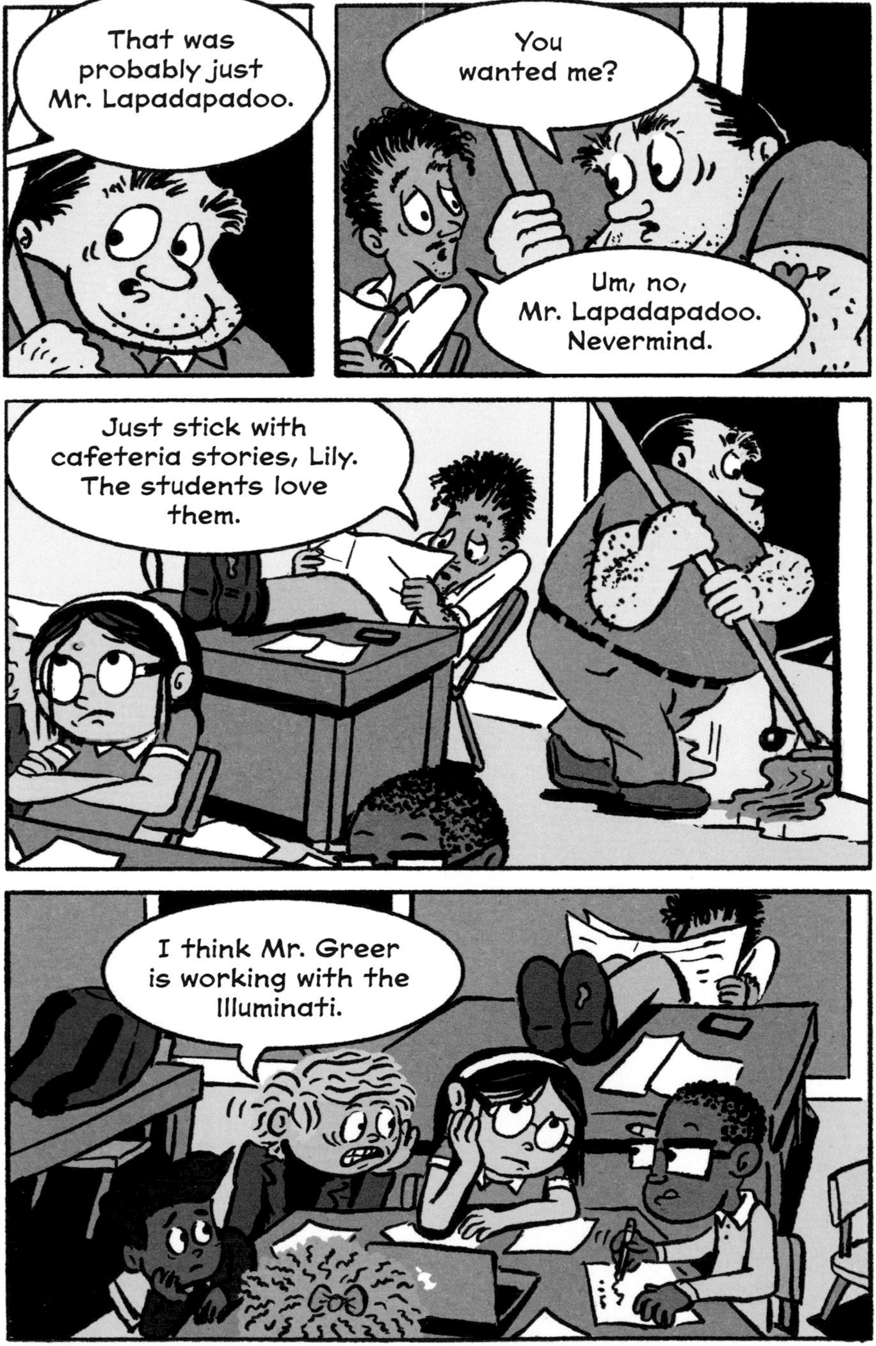
That was probably just Mr. Lapadapadoo.
You wanted me?
Um, no, Mr. Lapadapadoo. Nevermind.
Just stick with cafeteria stories, Lily. The students love them.
I think Mr. Greer is working with the Illuminati.

Mom, the neighbor kid is pressing his face against the window again.

I know.

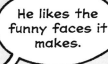

He likes the funny faces it makes.

Just pull the shade down and he'll go away.

What about you, Lily? Anything interesting happen at school today?

Some kids said they saw a yeti in the locker room.

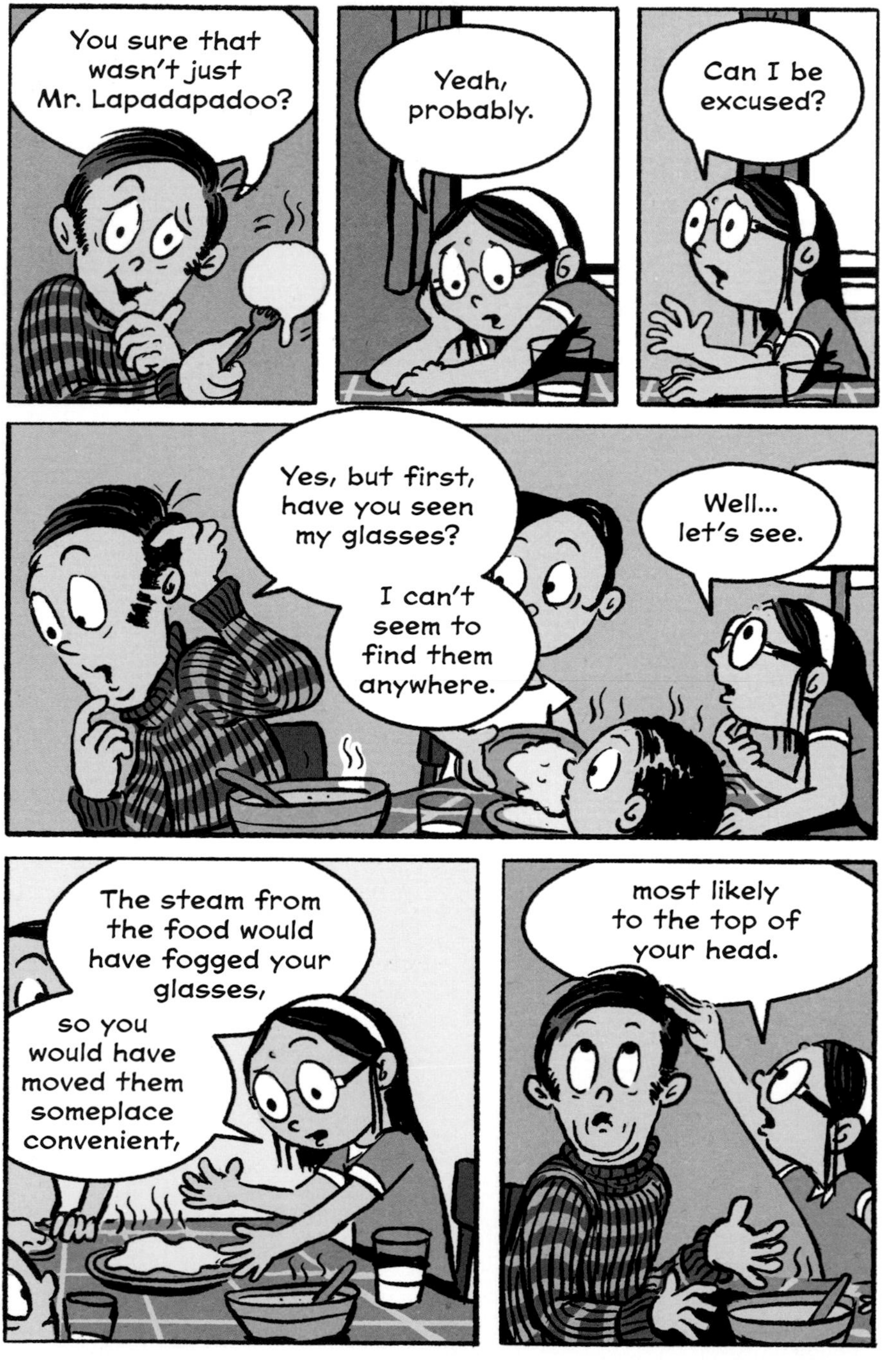
You sure that wasn't just Mr. Lapadapadoo?
Yeah, probably.
Can I be excused?
Yes, but first, have you seen my glasses?
I can't seem to find them anywhere.
Well... let's see.
The steam from the food would have fogged your glasses,
so you would have moved them someplace convenient,
most likely to the top of your head.

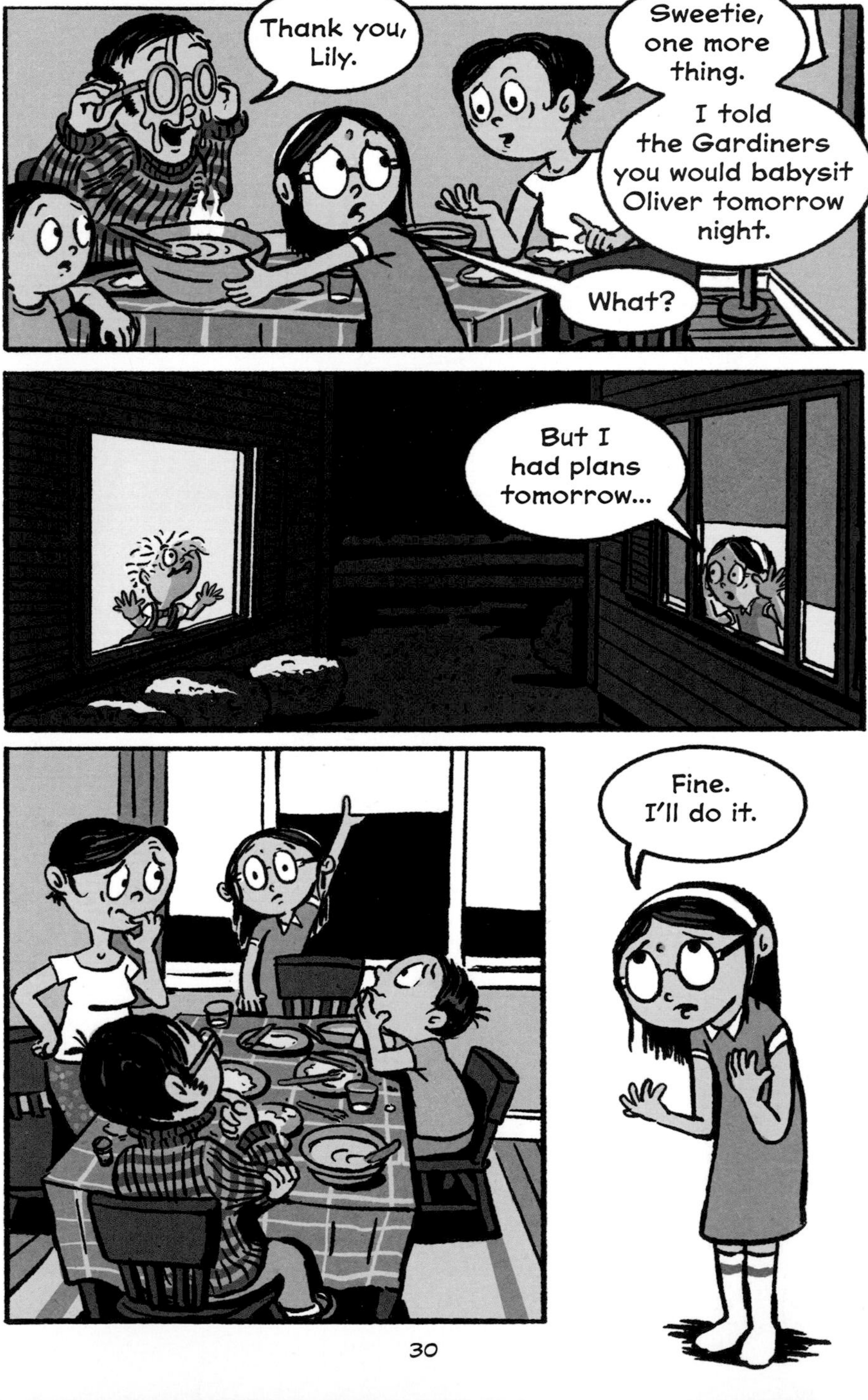
Thank you, Lily.
Sweetie, one more thing.
I told the Gardiners you would babysit Oliver tomorrow night.
What?
But I had plans tomorrow...
Fine. I'll do it.

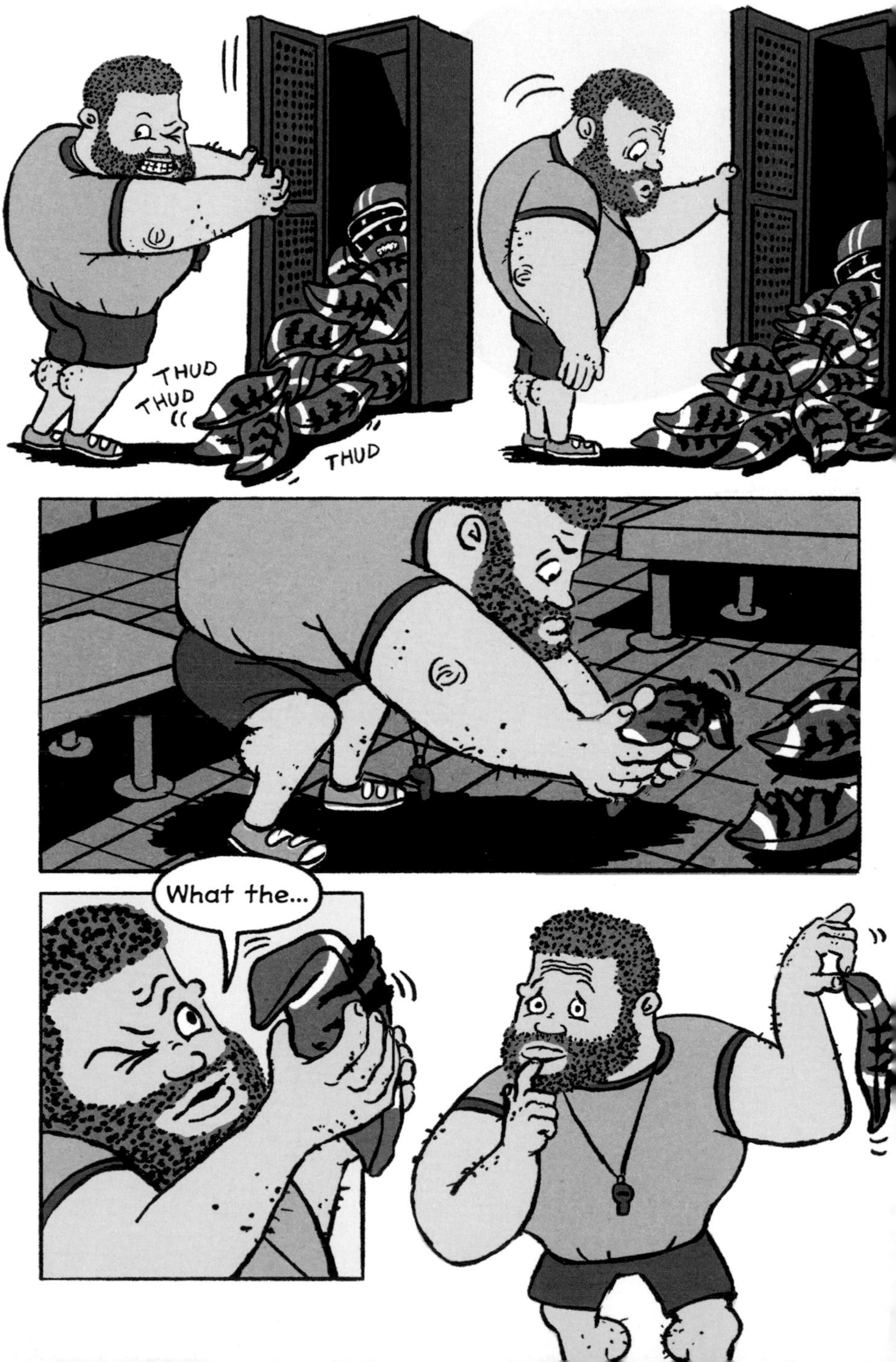
THUD
THUD
THUD
What the...

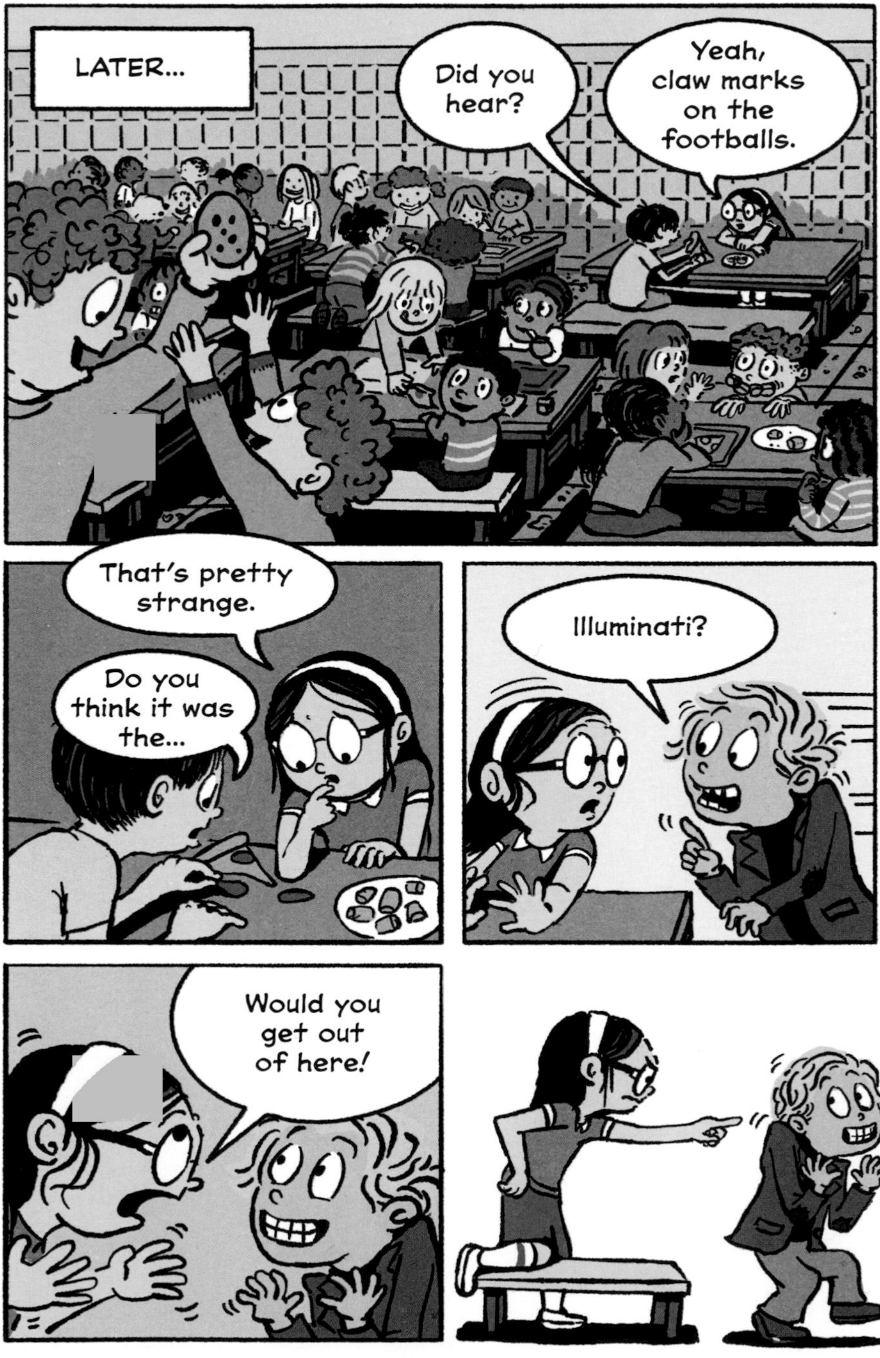
LATER...
Did you hear?
Yeah, claw marks on the footballs.
That's pretty strange.
Do you think it was the...
Illuminati?
Would you get out of here!

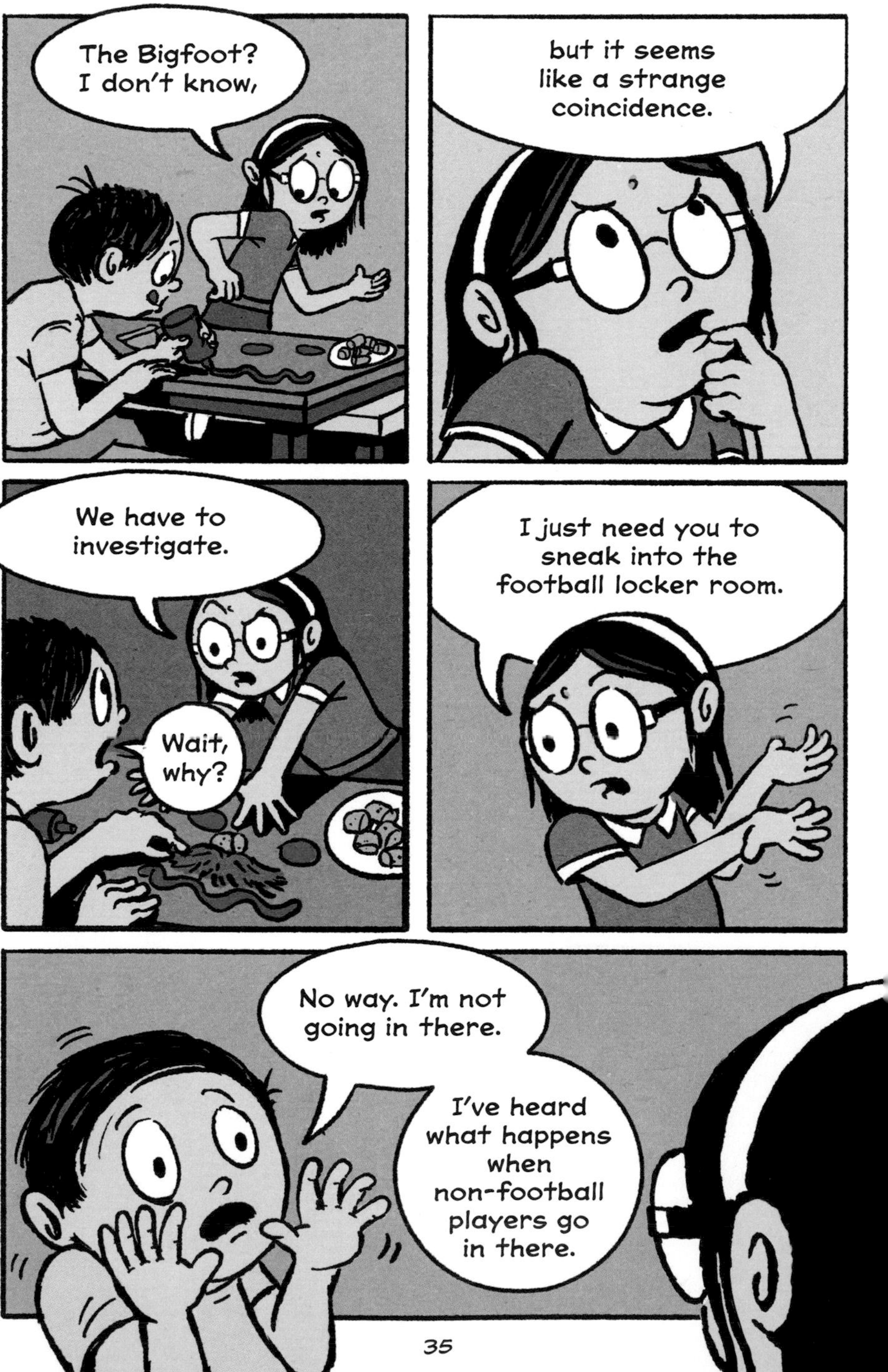
The Bigfoot? I don't know,
but it seems like a strange coincidence.
We have to investigate.
Wait, why?
I just need you to sneak into the football locker room.
No way. I'm not going in there.
I've heard what happens when non-football players go in there.

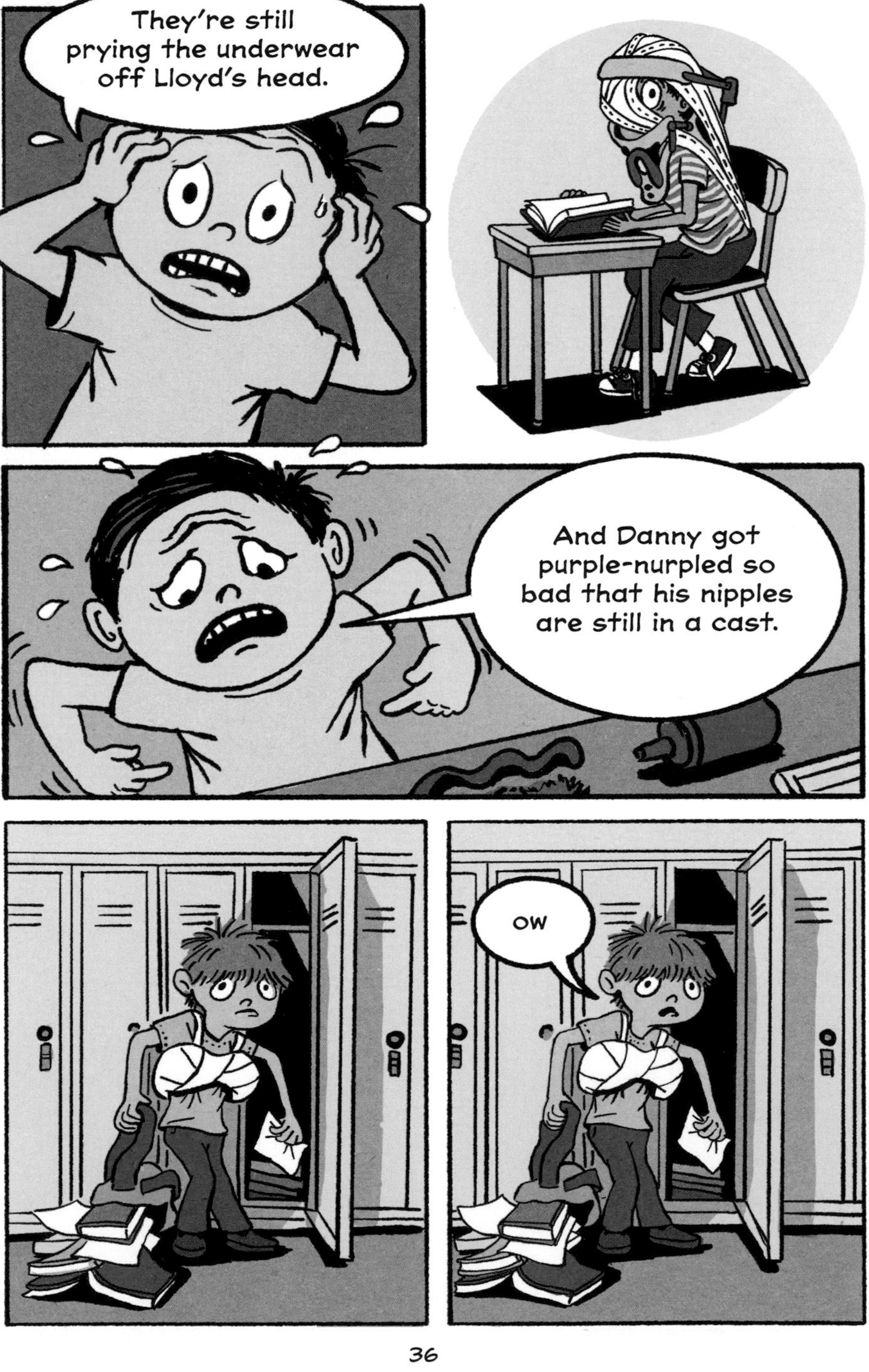
They're still prying the underwear off Lloyd's head.
And Danny got purple-nurpled so bad that his nipples are still in a cast.
OW

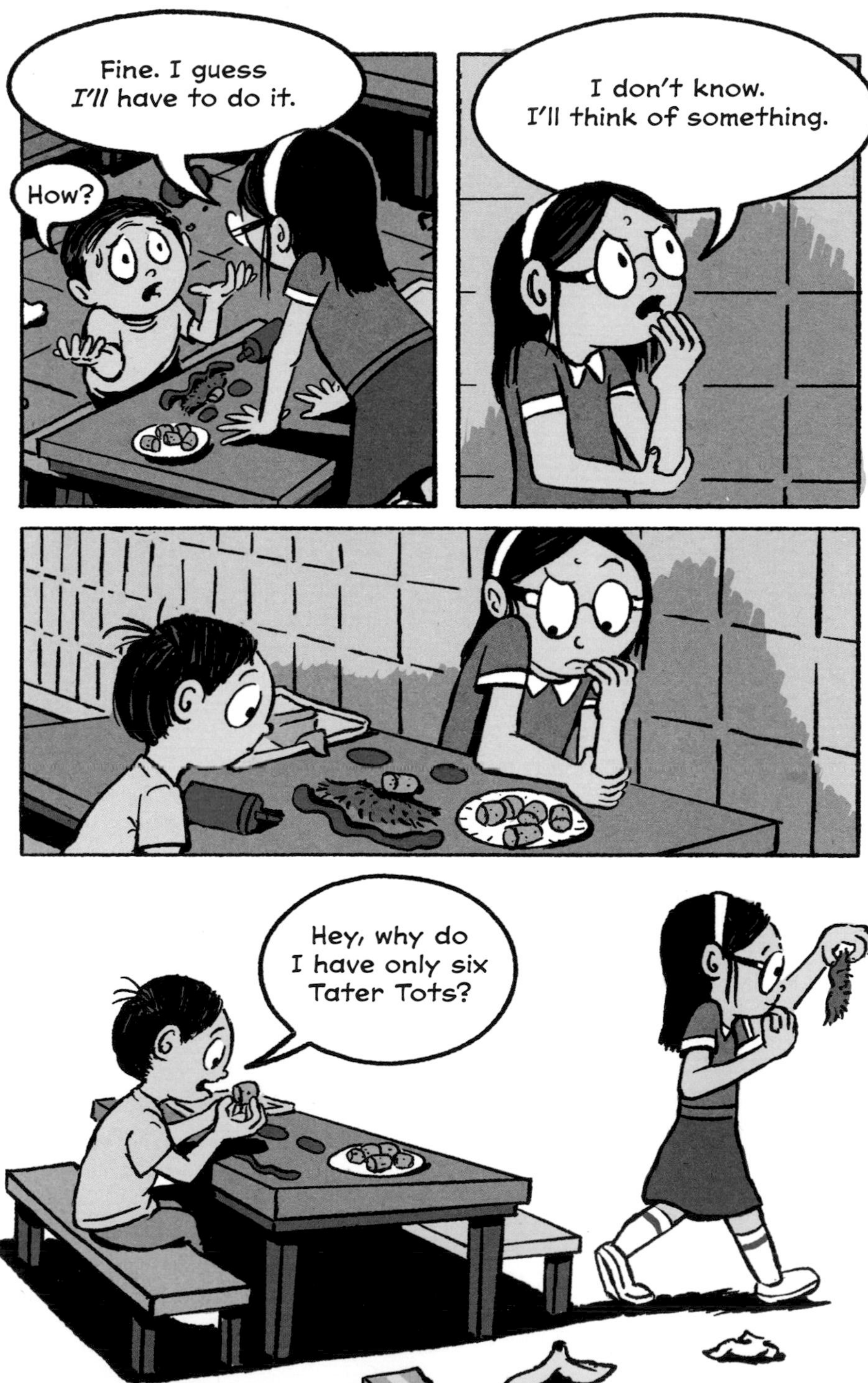
Fine. I guess *I'll* have to do it.
How?
I don't know. I'll think of something.
Hey, why do I have only six Tater Tots?

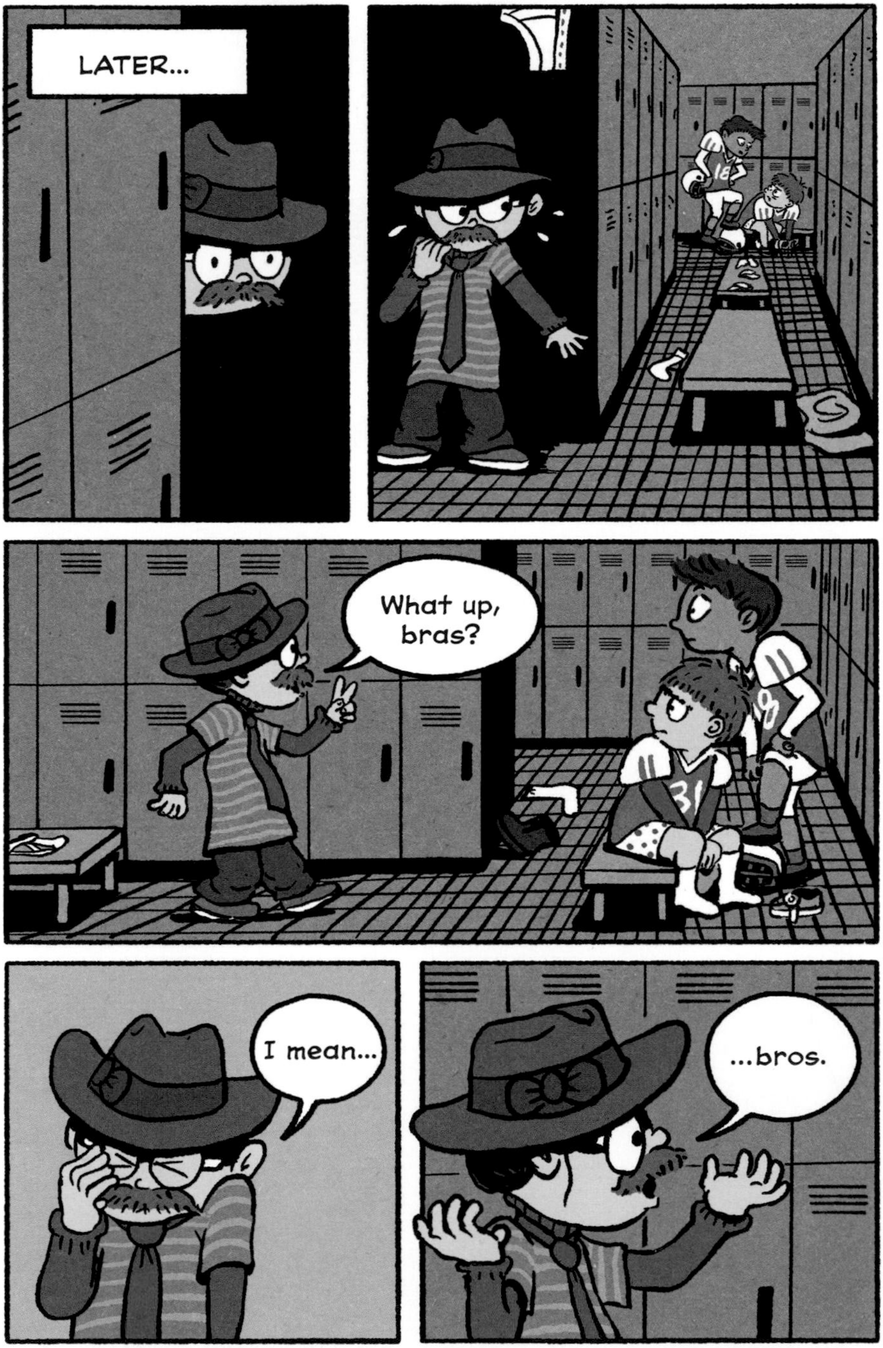
LATER...
What up, bras?
I mean...
...bros.

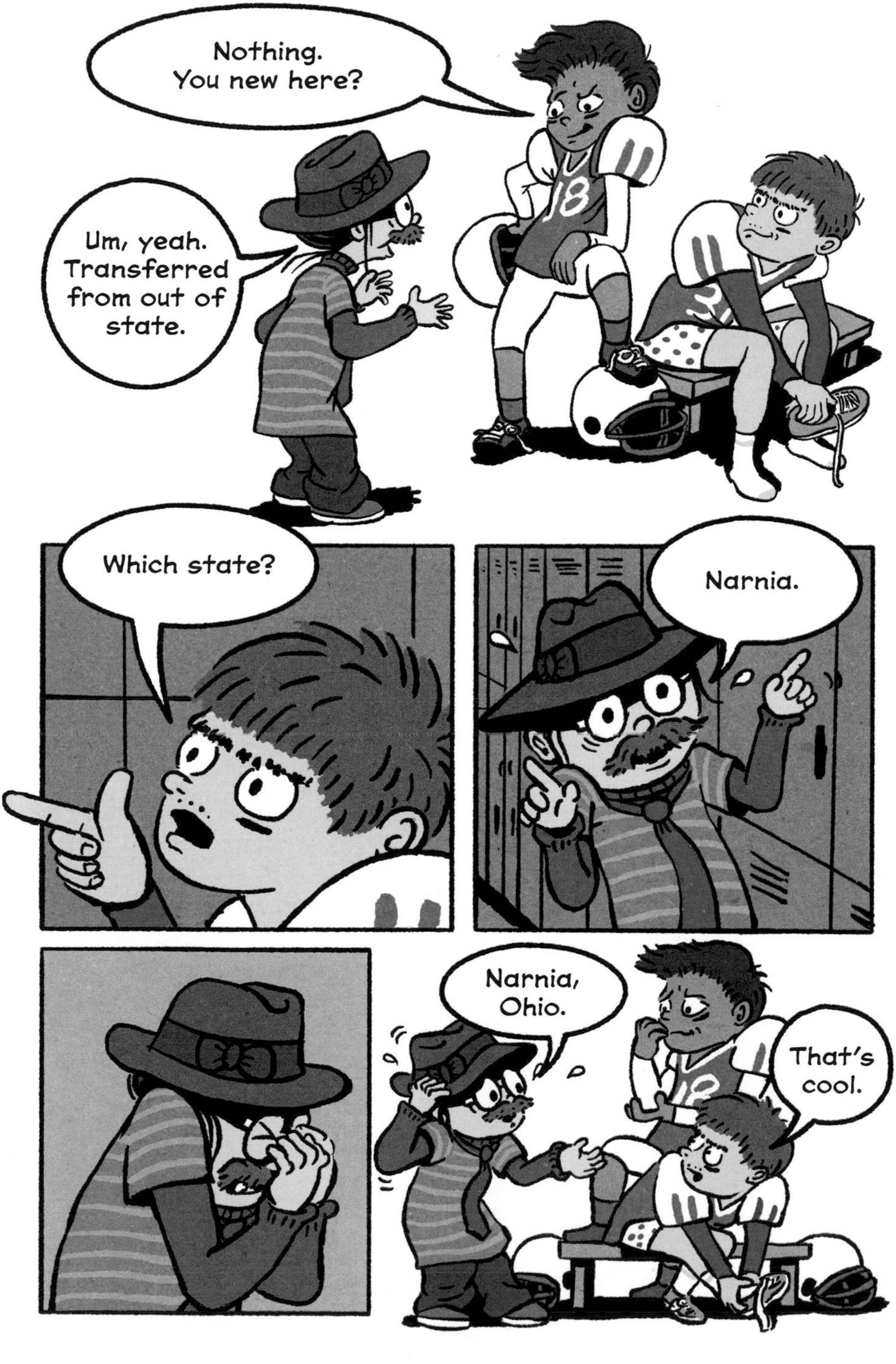
Nothing. You new here?
Um, yeah. Transferred from out of state.
Which state?
Narnia.
Narnia, Ohio.
That's cool.

40

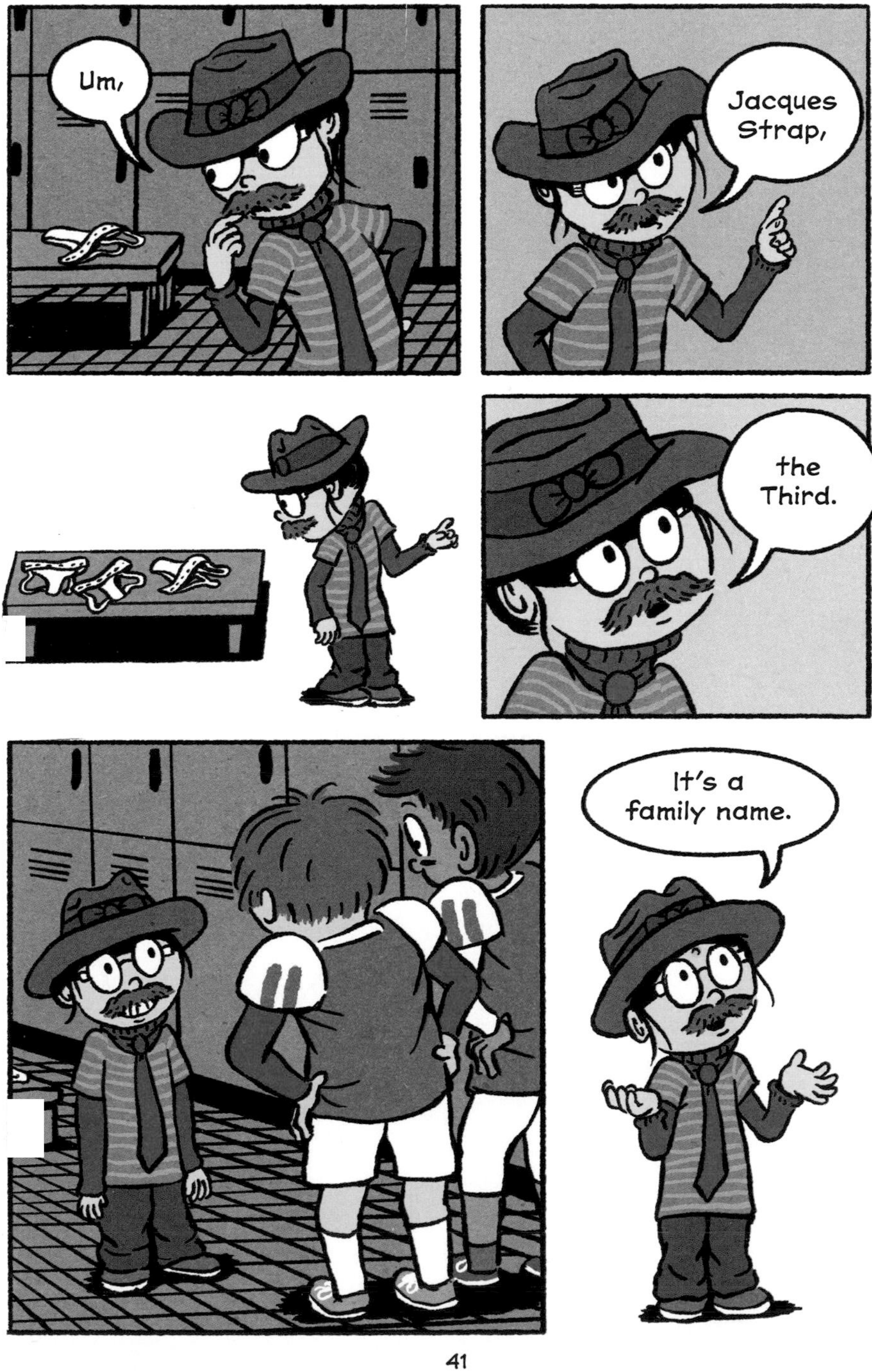
Um,
Jacques Strap,
the Third.
It's a family name.

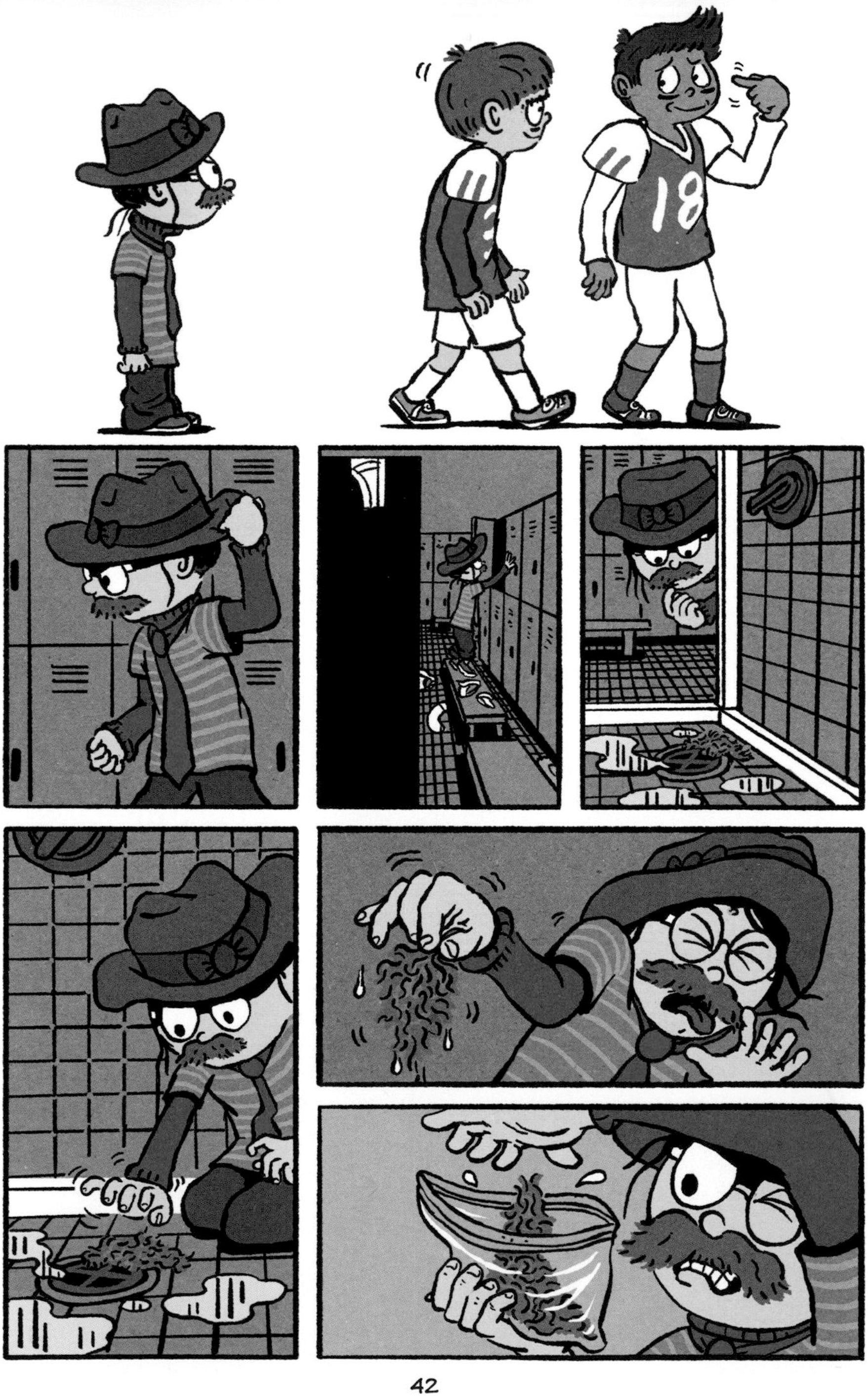

43

44

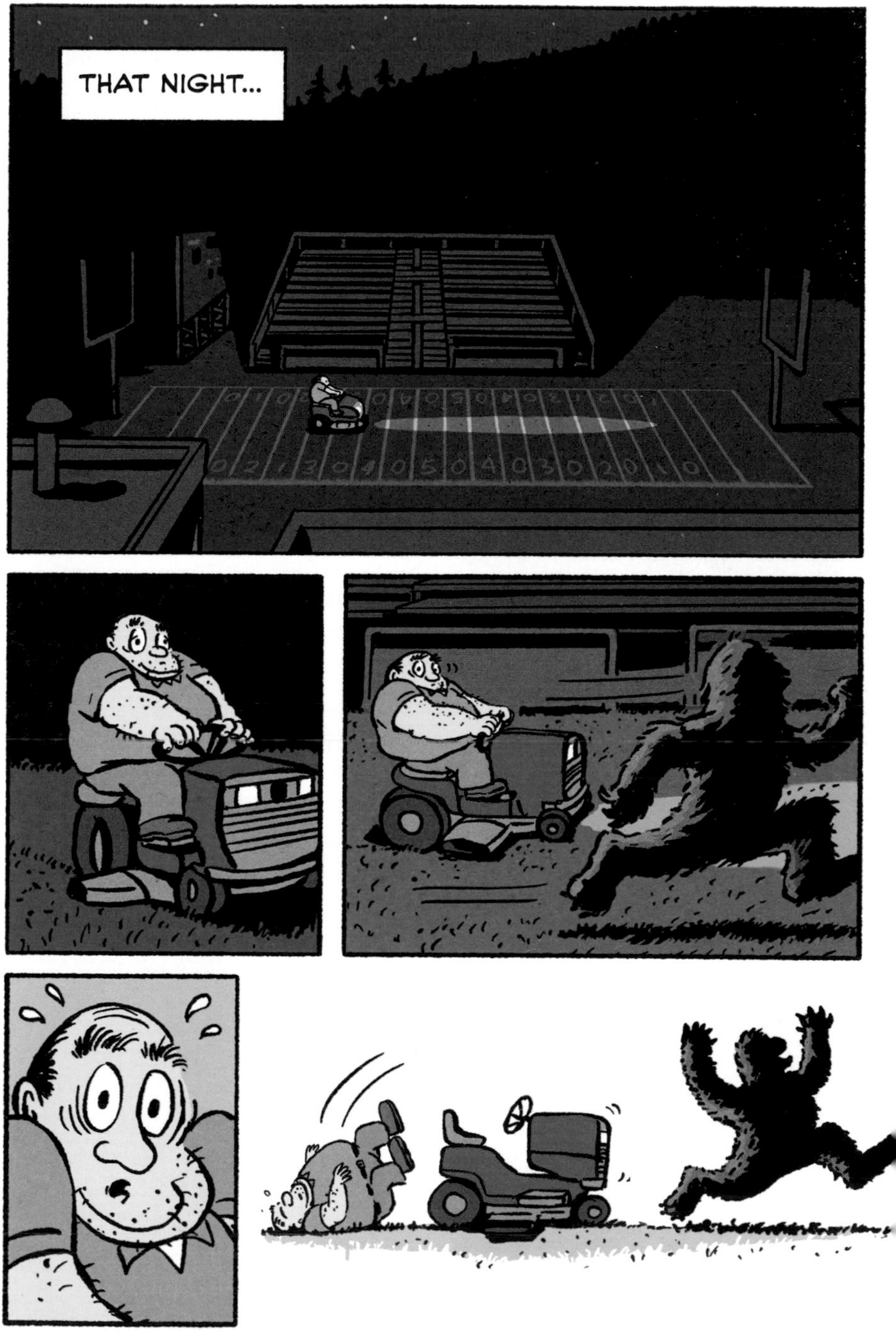
THAT NIGHT...

49

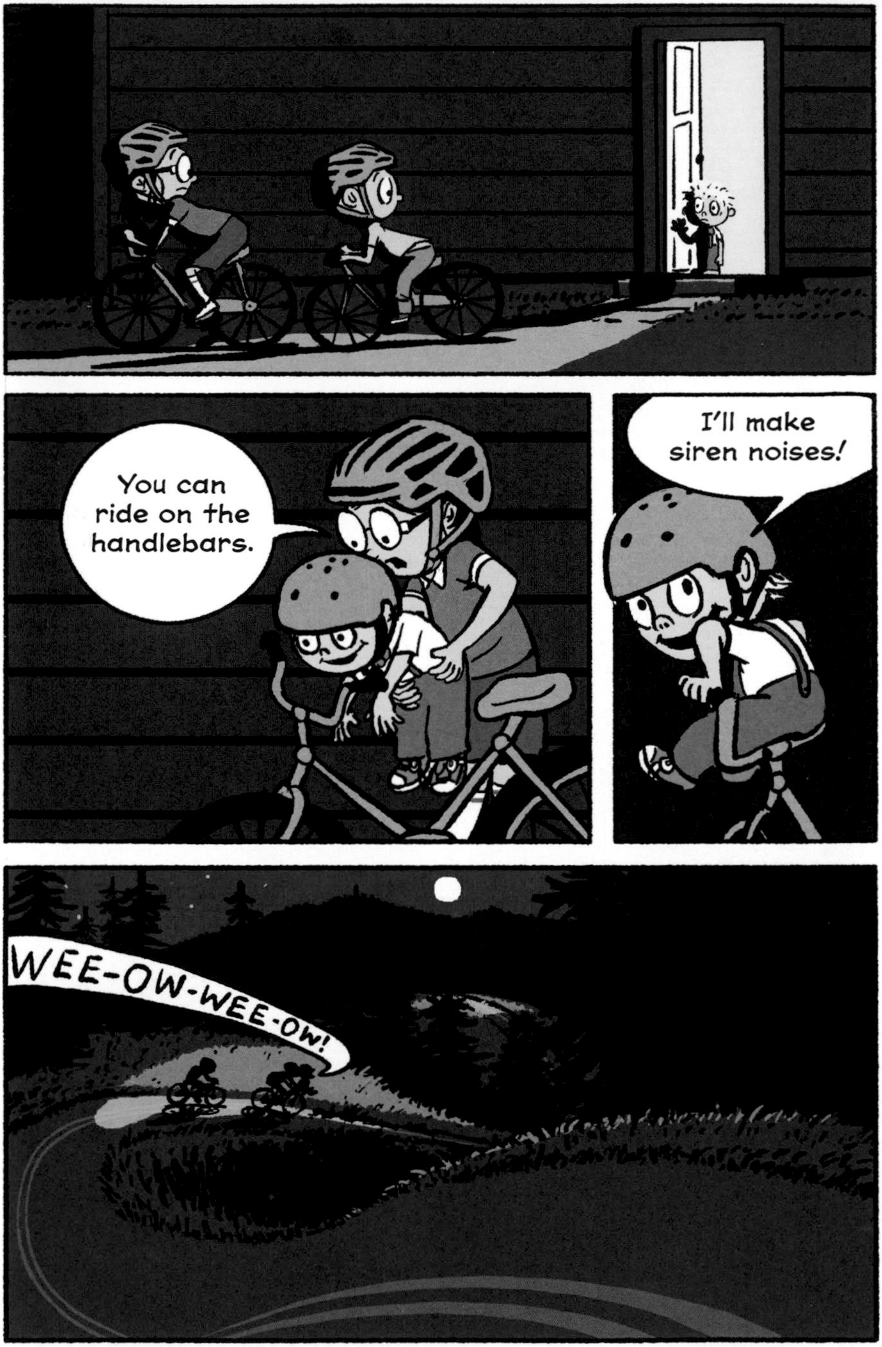
You can ride on the handlebars.
I'll make siren noises!
WEE-OW-WEE-OW!

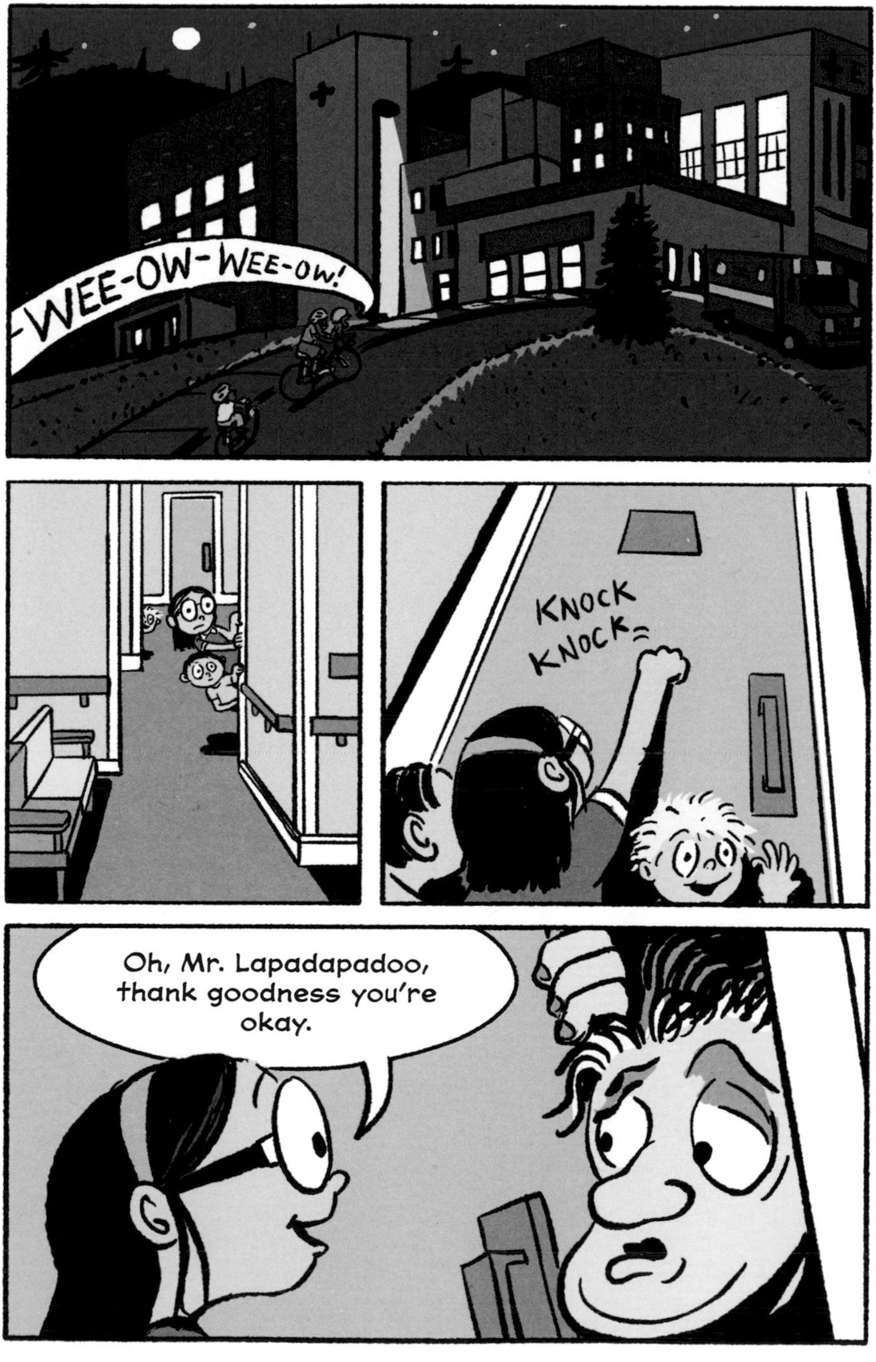
-WEE-OW-WEE-OW!
KNOCK
KNOCK
Oh, Mr. Lapadapadoo, thank goodness you're okay.

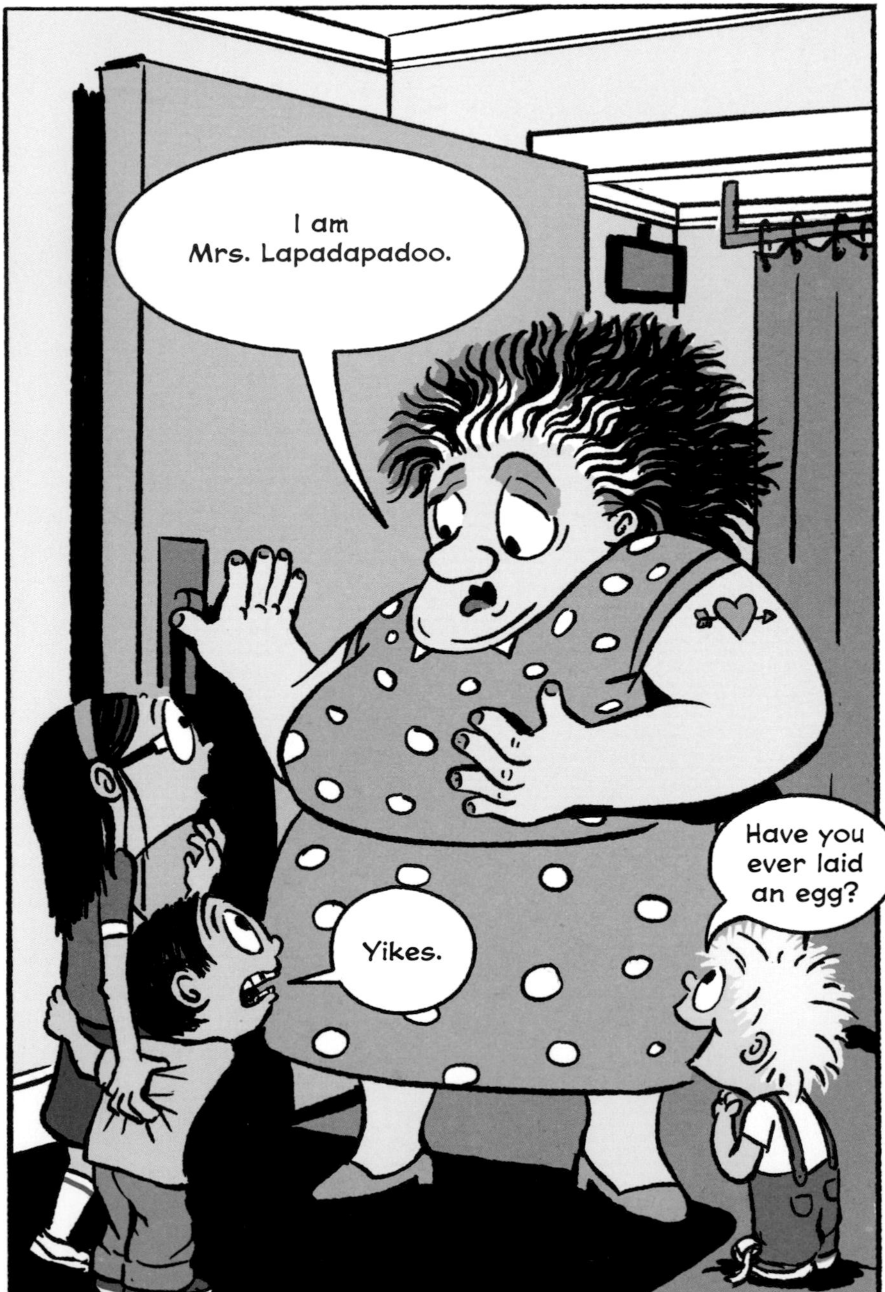
I am
Mrs. Lapadapadoo.
Yikes.
Have you
ever laid
an egg?

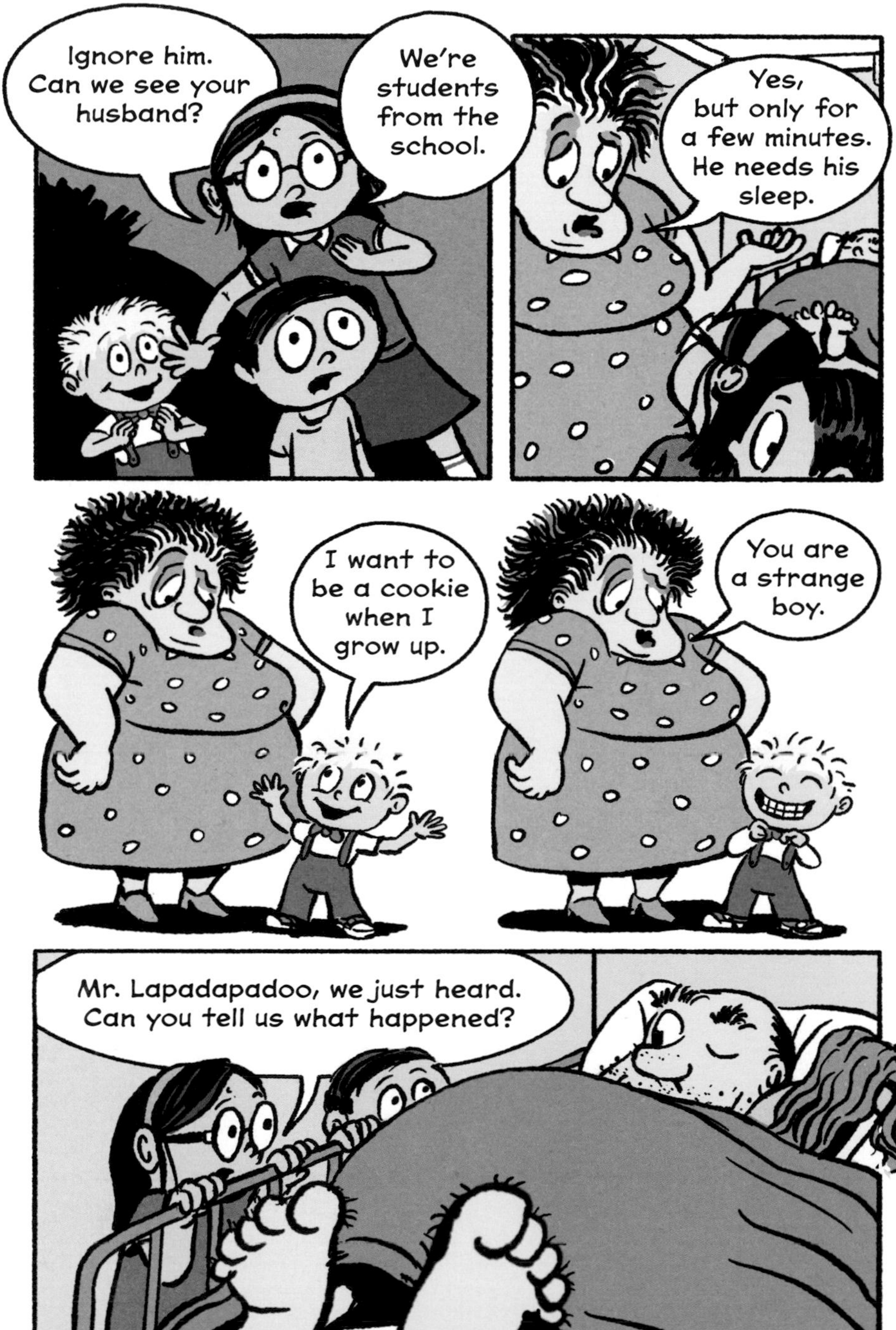
Ignore him. Can we see your husband?
We're students from the school.
Yes, but only for a few minutes. He needs his sleep.
I want to be a cookie when I grow up.
You are a strange boy.
Mr. Lapadapadoo, we just heard. Can you tell us what happened?

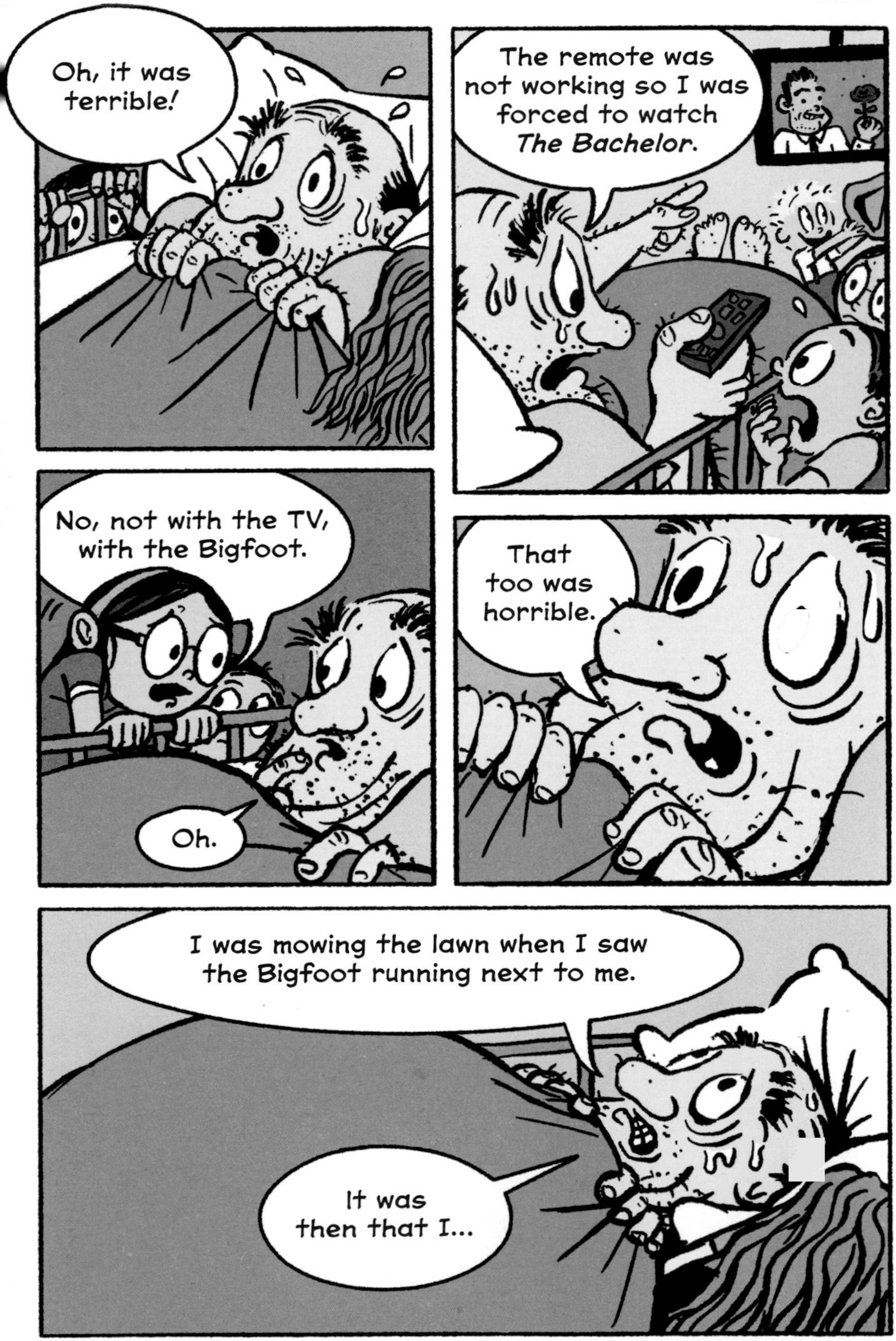

Oh, it was terrible!
The remote was not working so I was forced to watch *The Bachelor*.
No, not with the TV, with the Bigfoot.
Oh.
That too was horrible.
I was mowing the lawn when I saw the Bigfoot running next to me.
It was then that I...

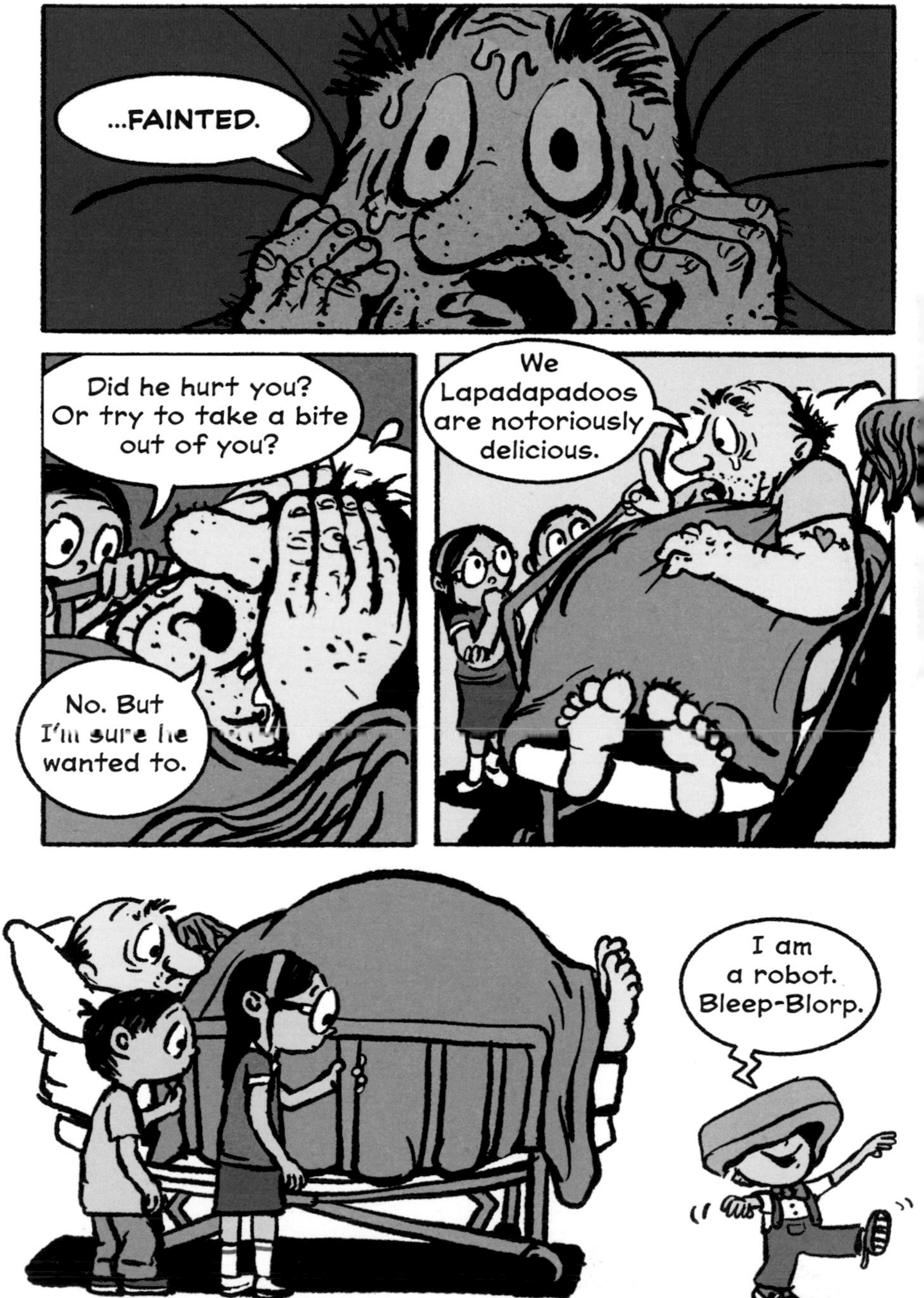
...FAINTED.
Did he hurt you? Or try to take a bite out of you?
No. But I'm sure he wanted to.
We Lapadapadoos are notoriously delicious.
I am a robot. Bleep-Blorp.

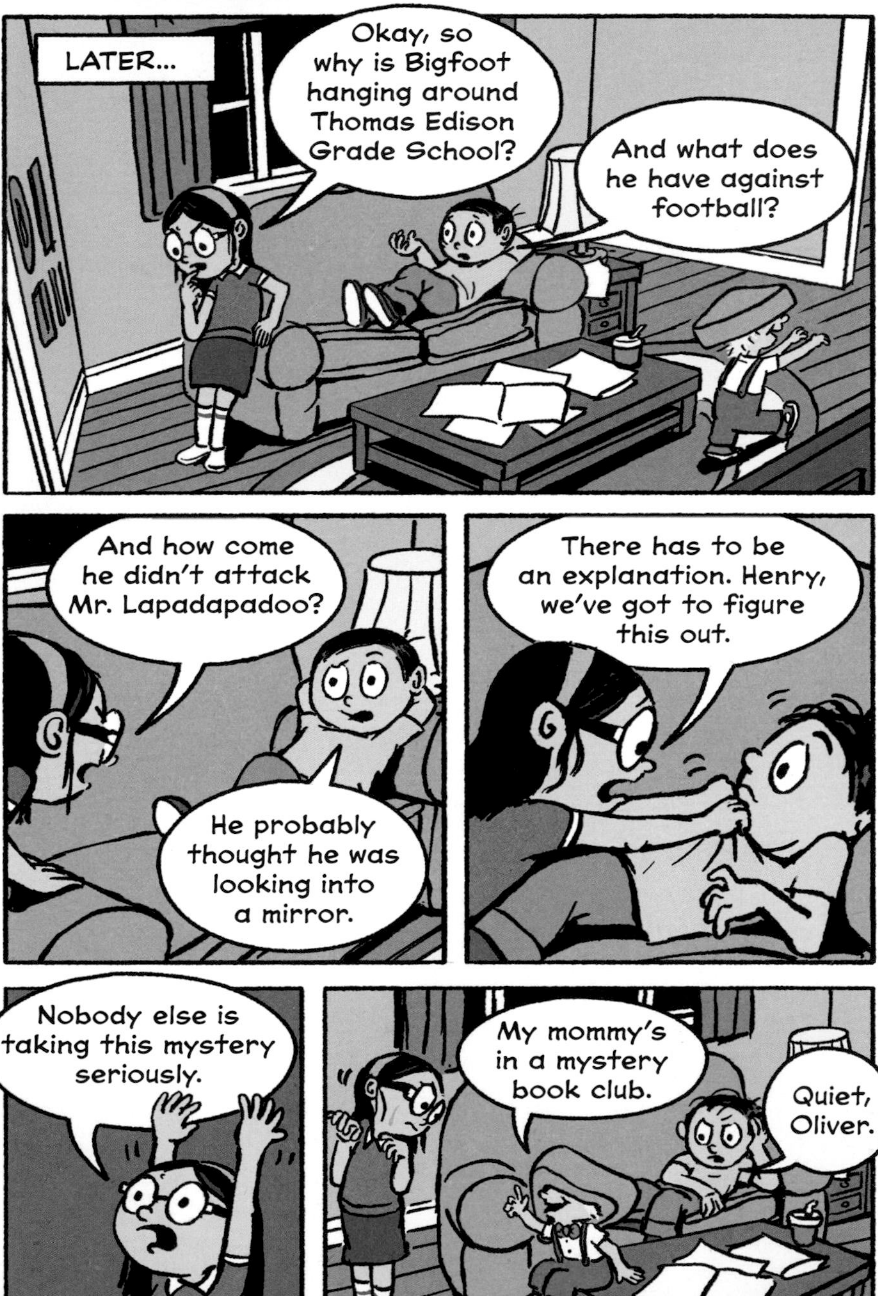
LATER...
Okay, so why is Bigfoot hanging around Thomas Edison Grade School?
And what does he have against football?
And how come he didn't attack Mr. Lapadapadoo?
He probably thought he was looking into a mirror.
There has to be an explanation. Henry, we've got to figure this out.
Nobody else is taking this mystery seriously.
My mommy's in a mystery book club.
Quiet, Oliver.

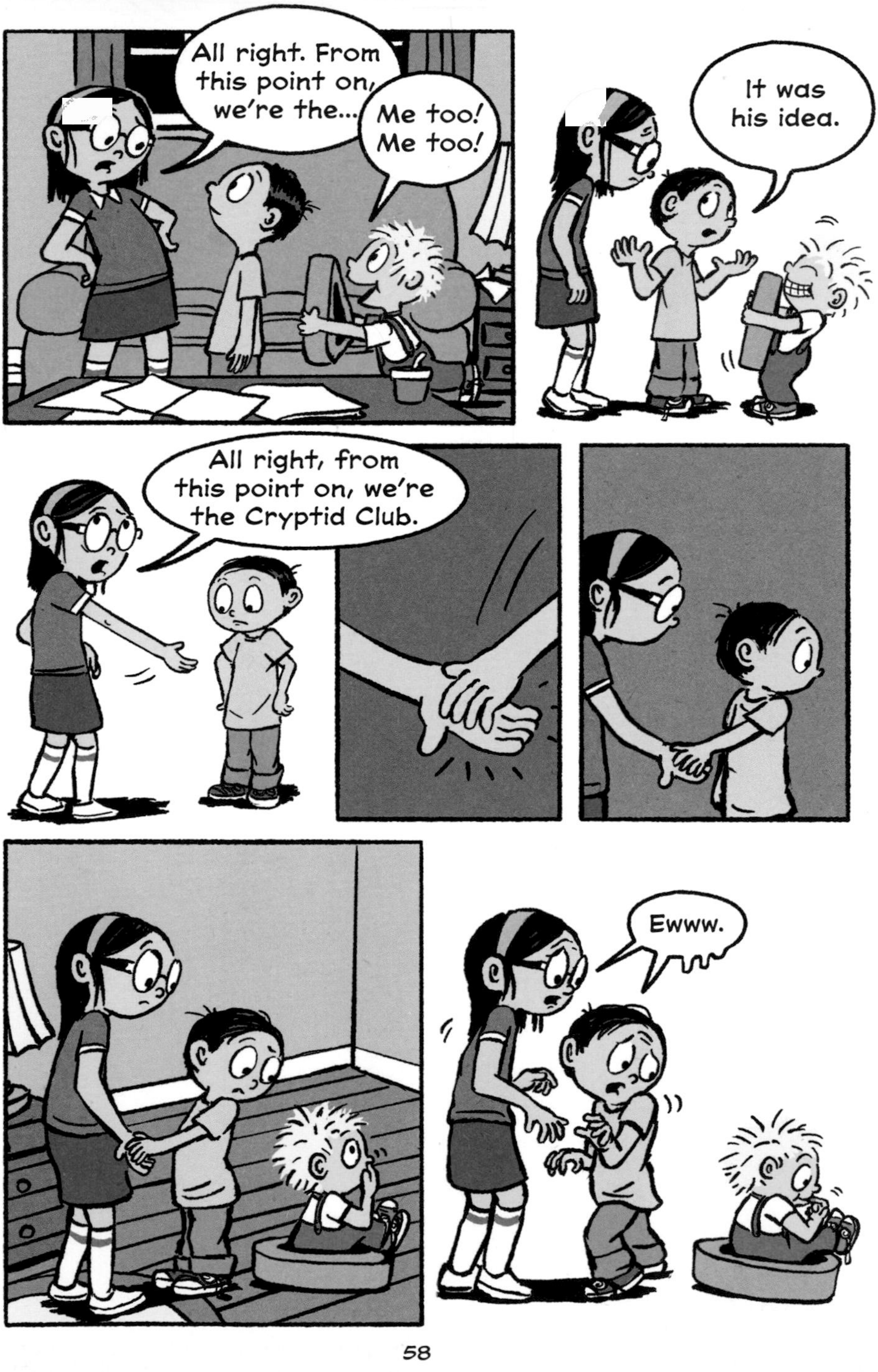
All right. From this point on, we're the...
Me too! Me too!
It was his idea.
All right, from this point on, we're the Cryptid Club.
Ewww.

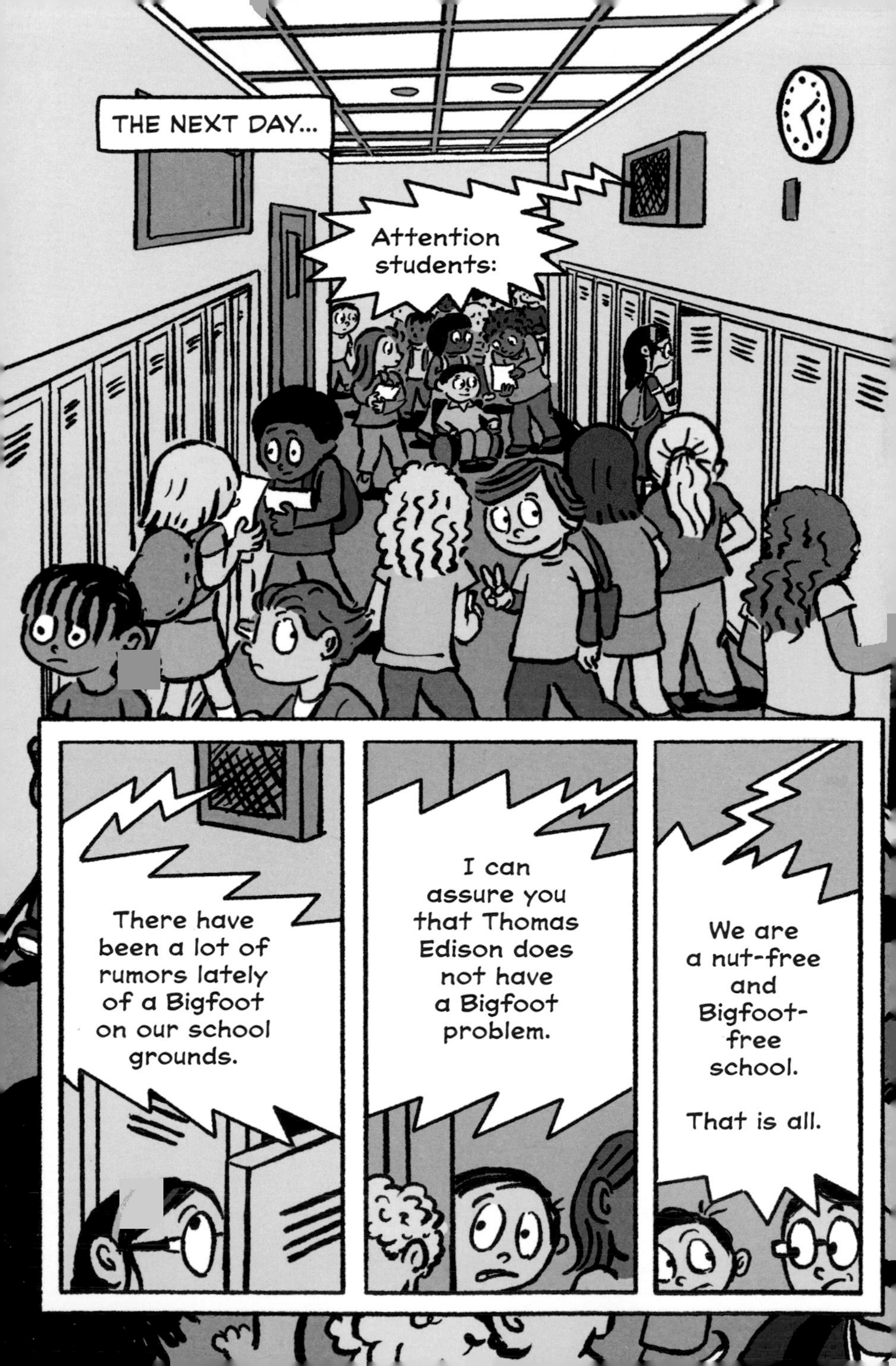
THE NEXT DAY...
Attention students:
There have been a lot of rumors lately of a Bigfoot on our school grounds.
I can assure you that Thomas Edison does not have a Bigfoot problem.
We are a nut-free and Bigfoot-free school.
That is all.

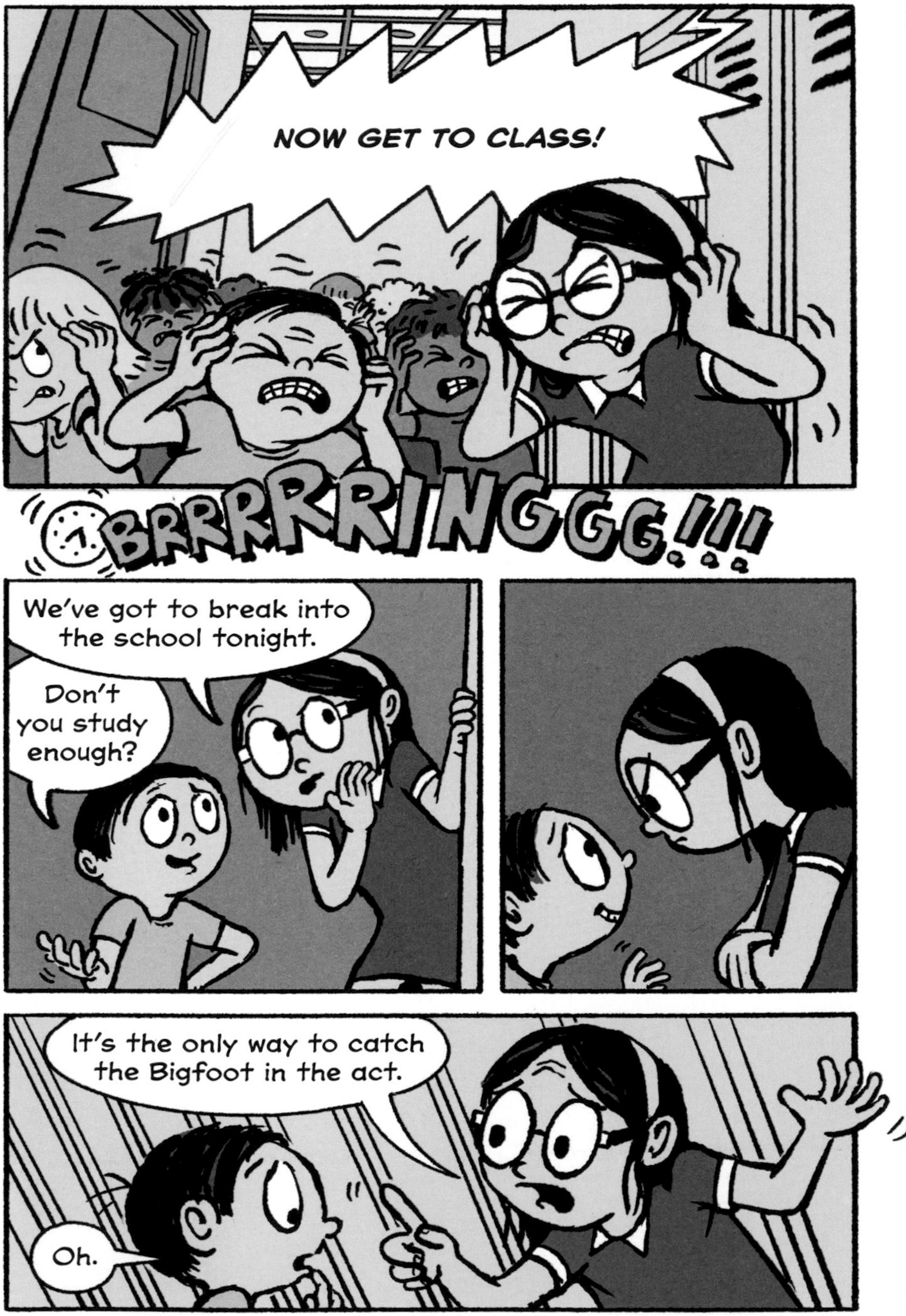
NOW GET TO CLASS!
BRRRRRRINGGG!!!
We've got to break into the school tonight.
Don't you study enough?
It's the only way to catch the Bigfoot in the act.
Oh.

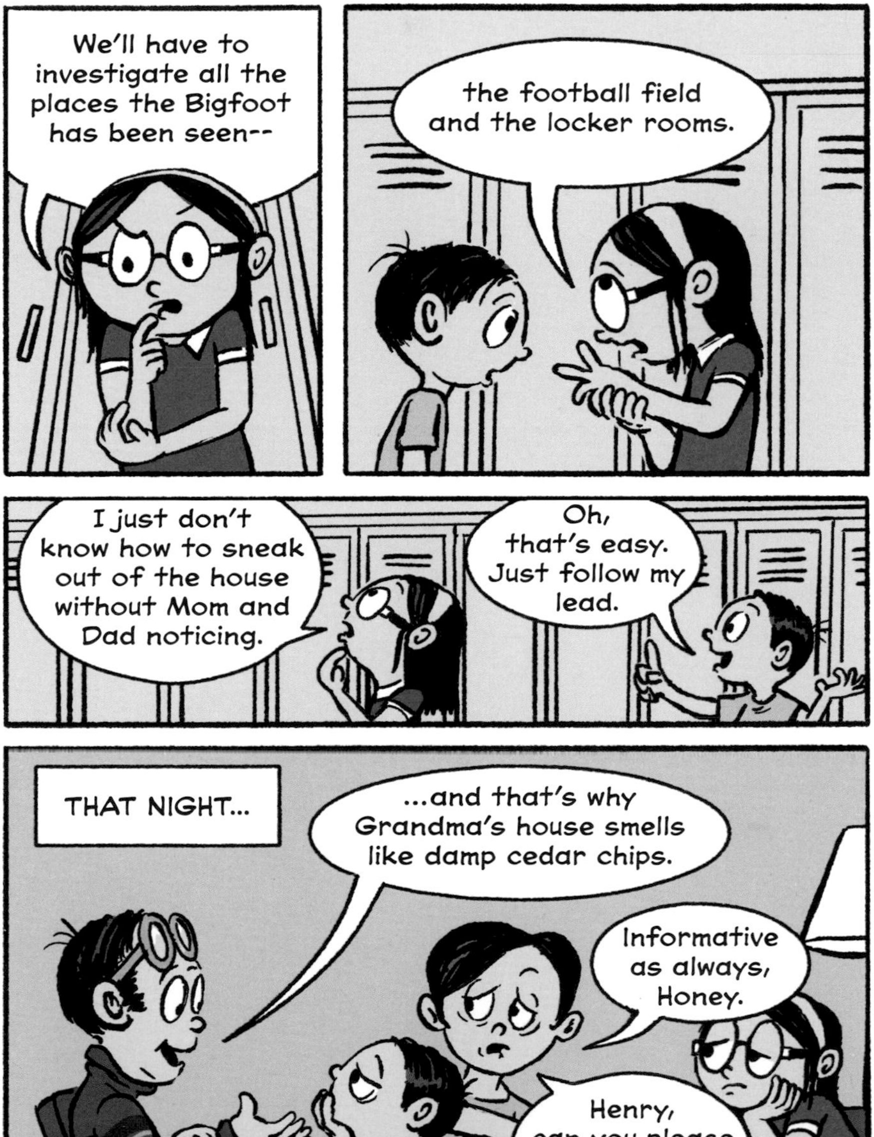
We'll have to investigate all the places the Bigfoot has been seen--
the football field and the locker rooms.
I just don't know how to sneak out of the house without Mom and Dad noticing.
Oh, that's easy. Just follow my lead.
THAT NIGHT...
...and that's why Grandma's house smells like damp cedar chips.
Informative as always, Honey.
Henry, can you please pass the gravy boat?

I am sorry, Mother, but I can't pass the gravy boat.

For I must go down with the ship.

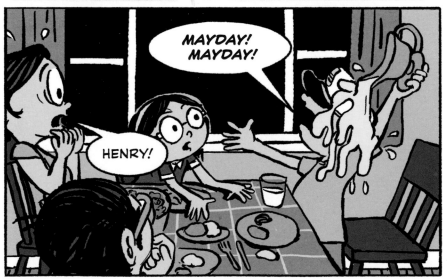

MAYDAY! MAYDAY!

HENRY!

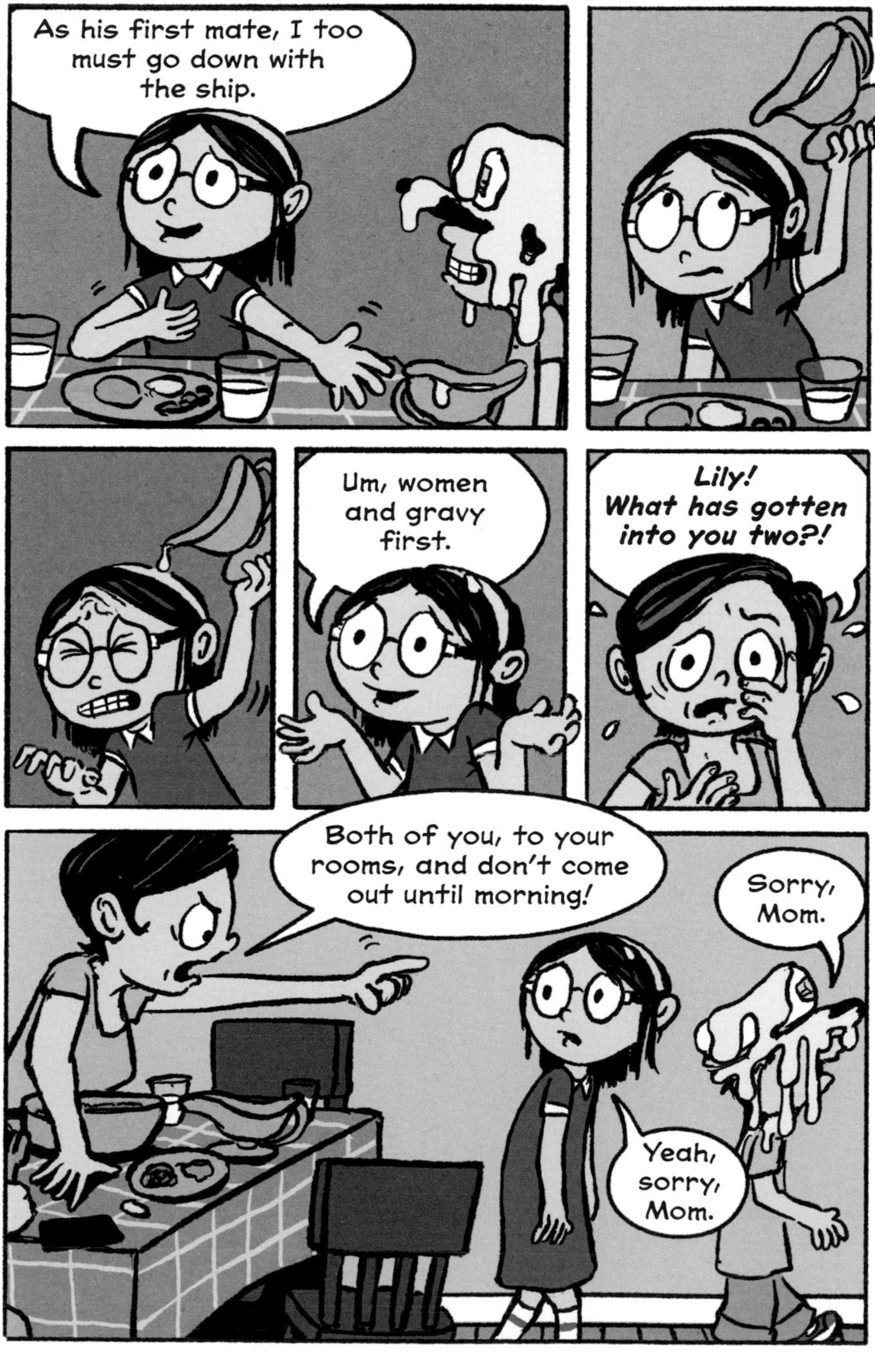
As his first mate, I too must go down with the ship.
Um, women and gravy first.
Lily! What has gotten into you two?!
Both of you, to your rooms, and don't come out until morning!
Sorry, Mom.
Yeah, sorry, Mom.

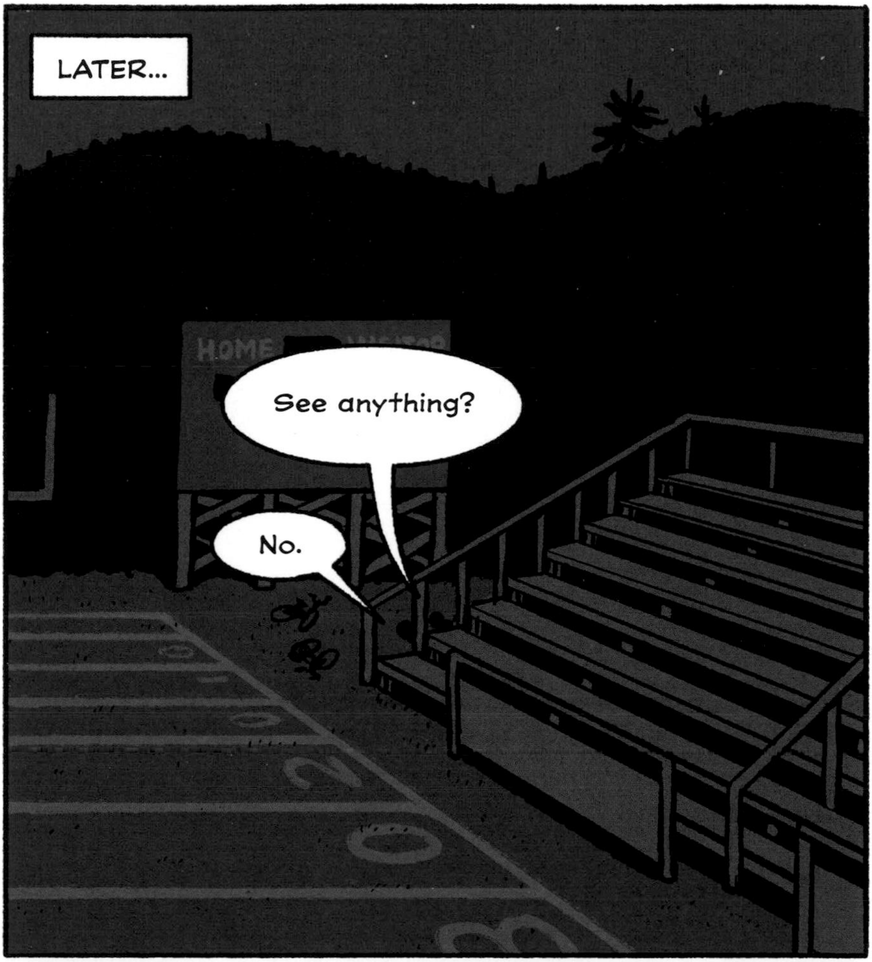
LATER...
HOME
See anything?
No.

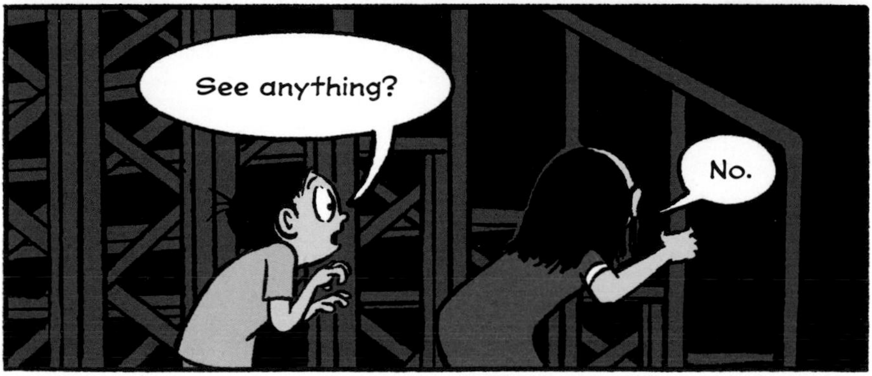
See anything?
No.

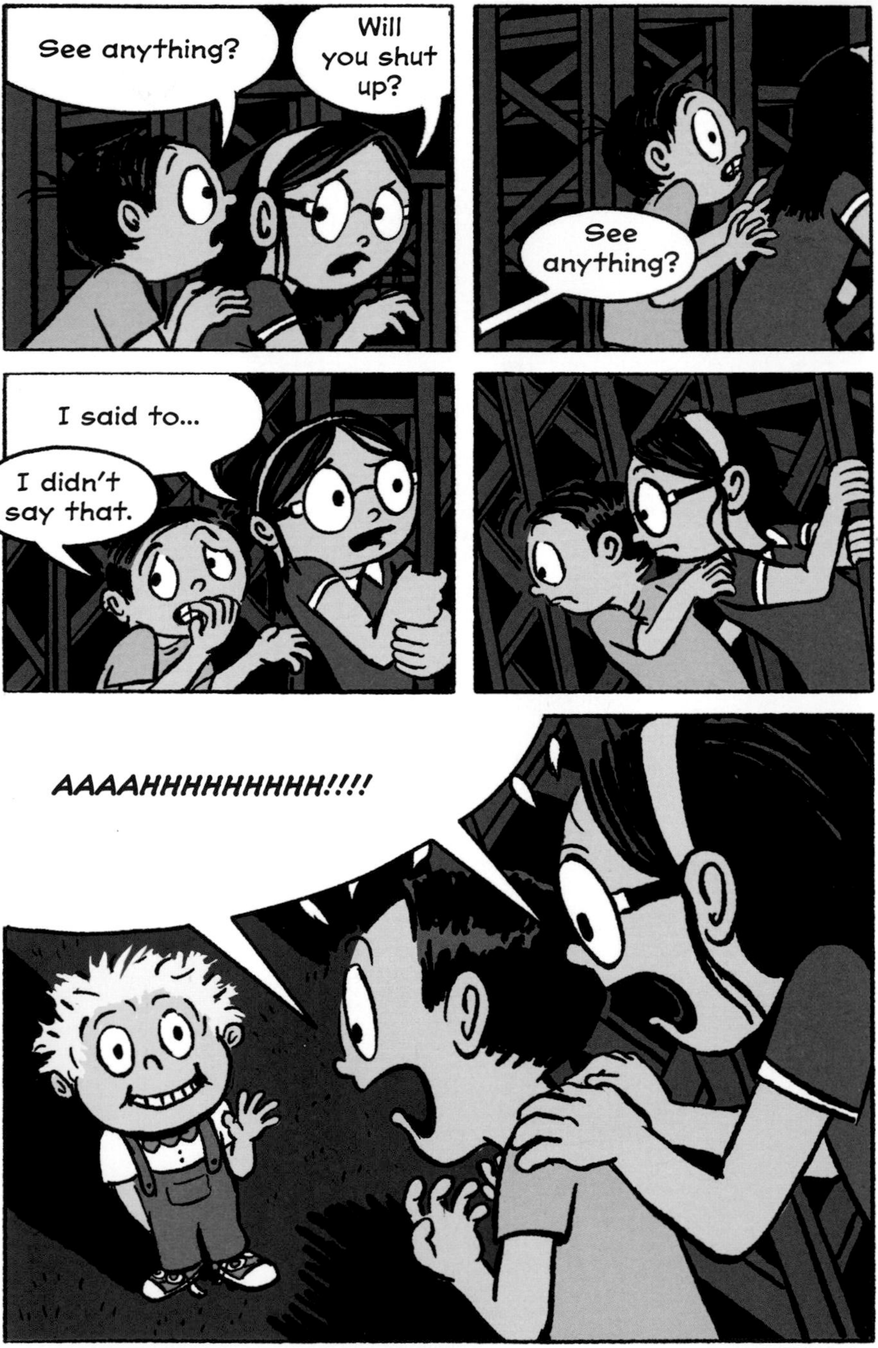
See anything?
Will you shut up?
See anything?
I said to...
I didn't say that.
AAAAHHHHHHHHHH!!!!

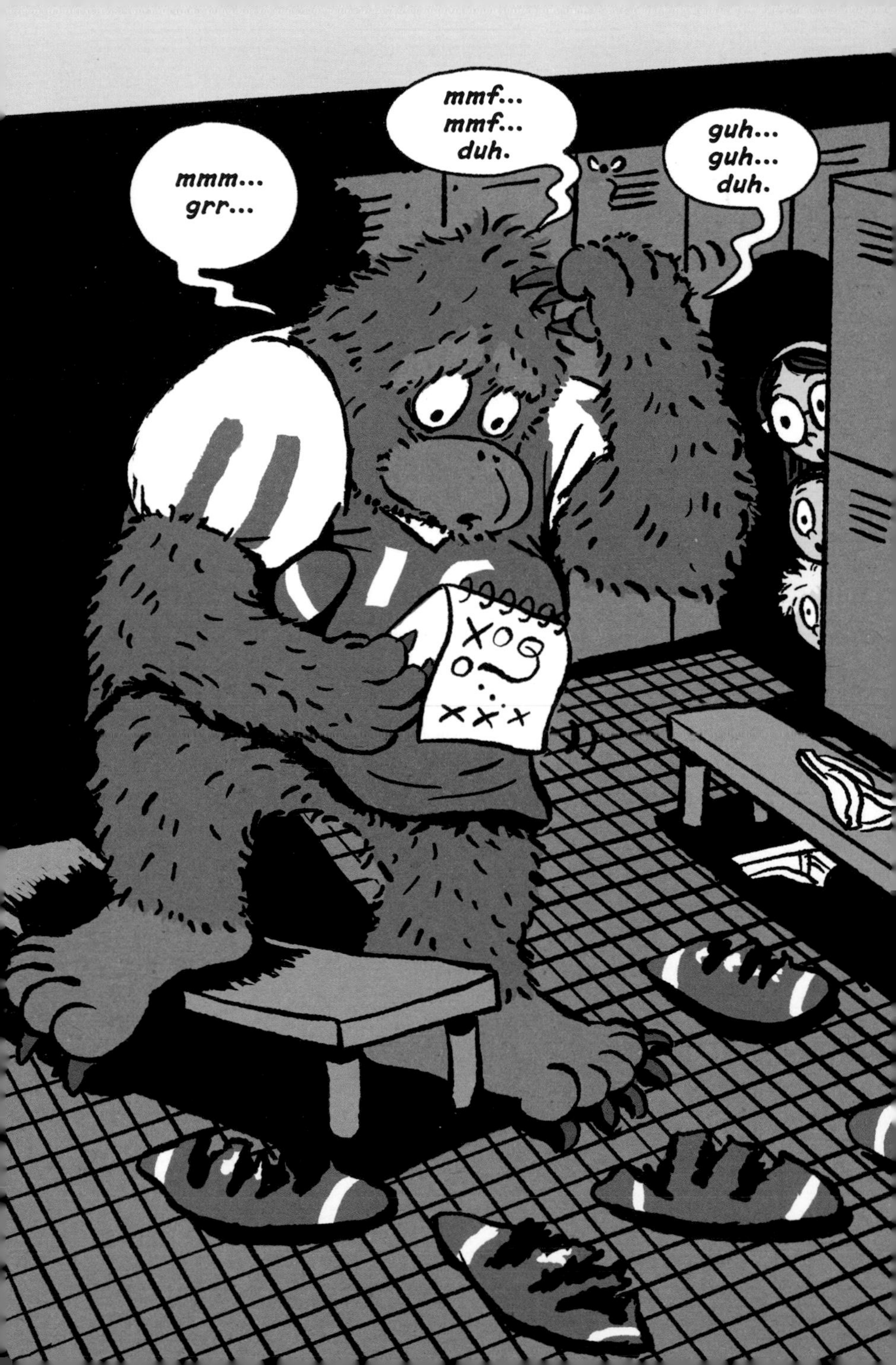
mmm... grrr...
mmf... mmf... duh.
guh... guh... duh.

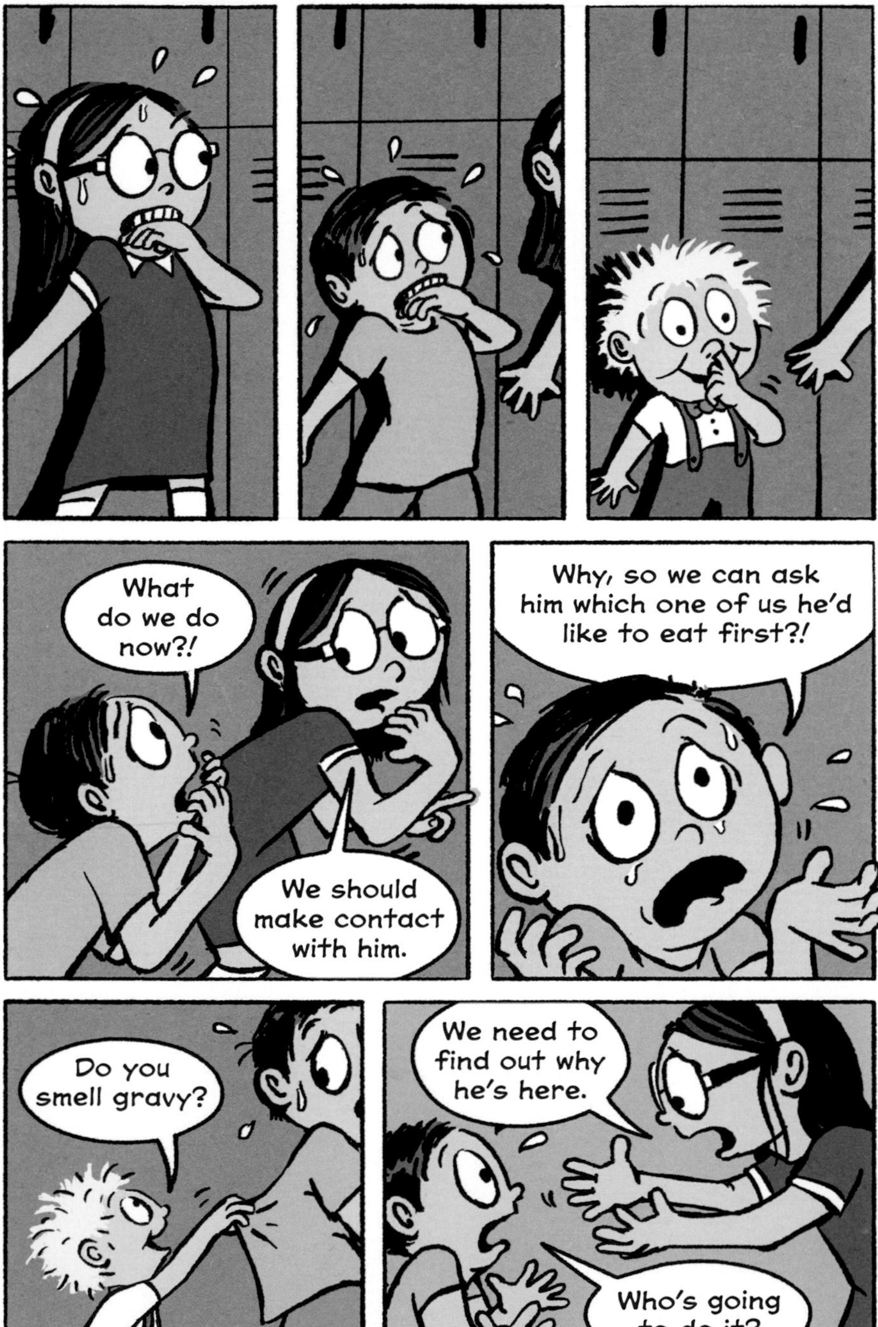
What do we do now?!
We should make contact with him.
Why, so we can ask him which one of us he'd like to eat first?!
Do you smell gravy?
We need to find out why he's here.
Who's going to do it?

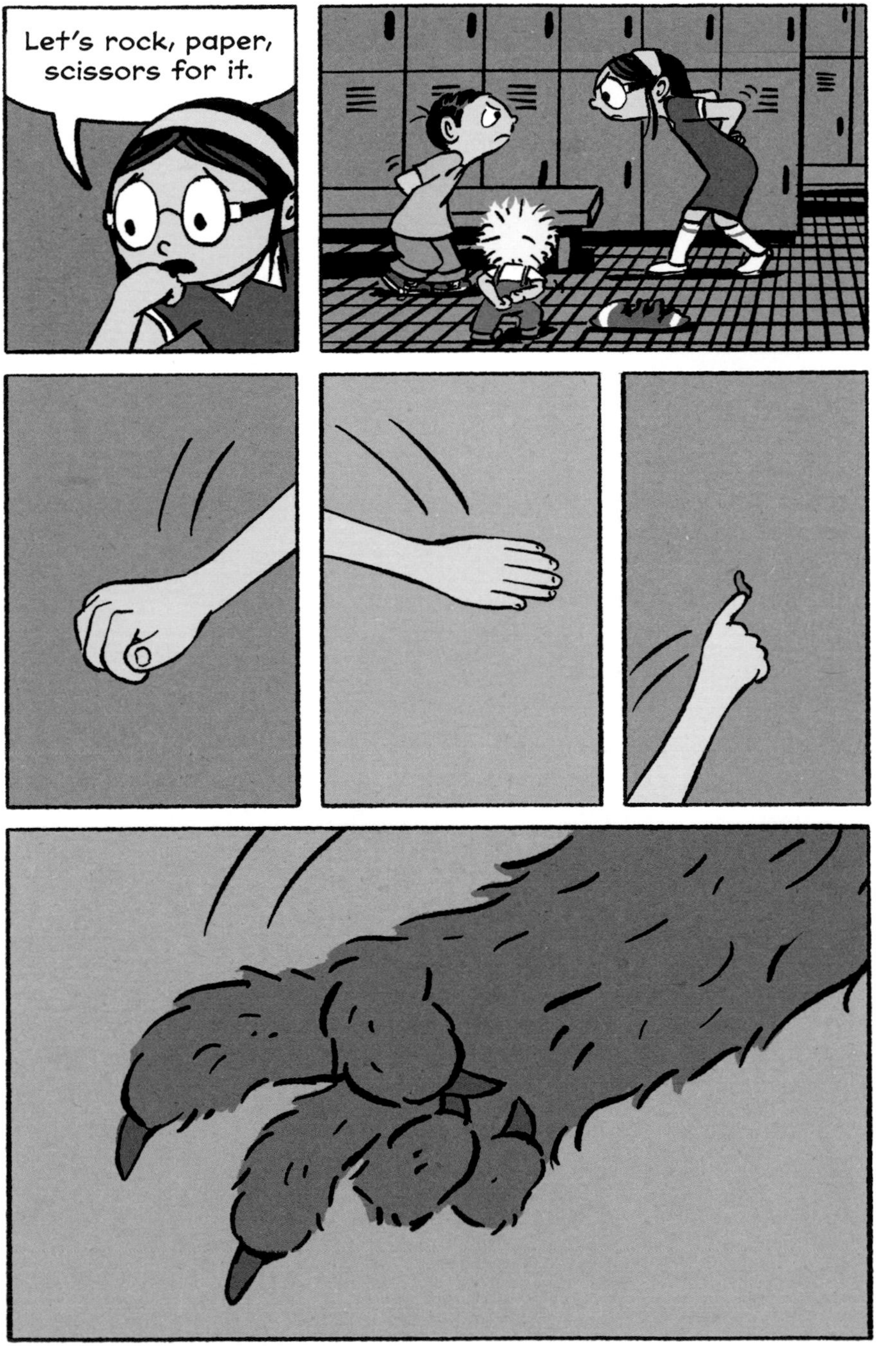
Let's rock, paper, scissors for it.

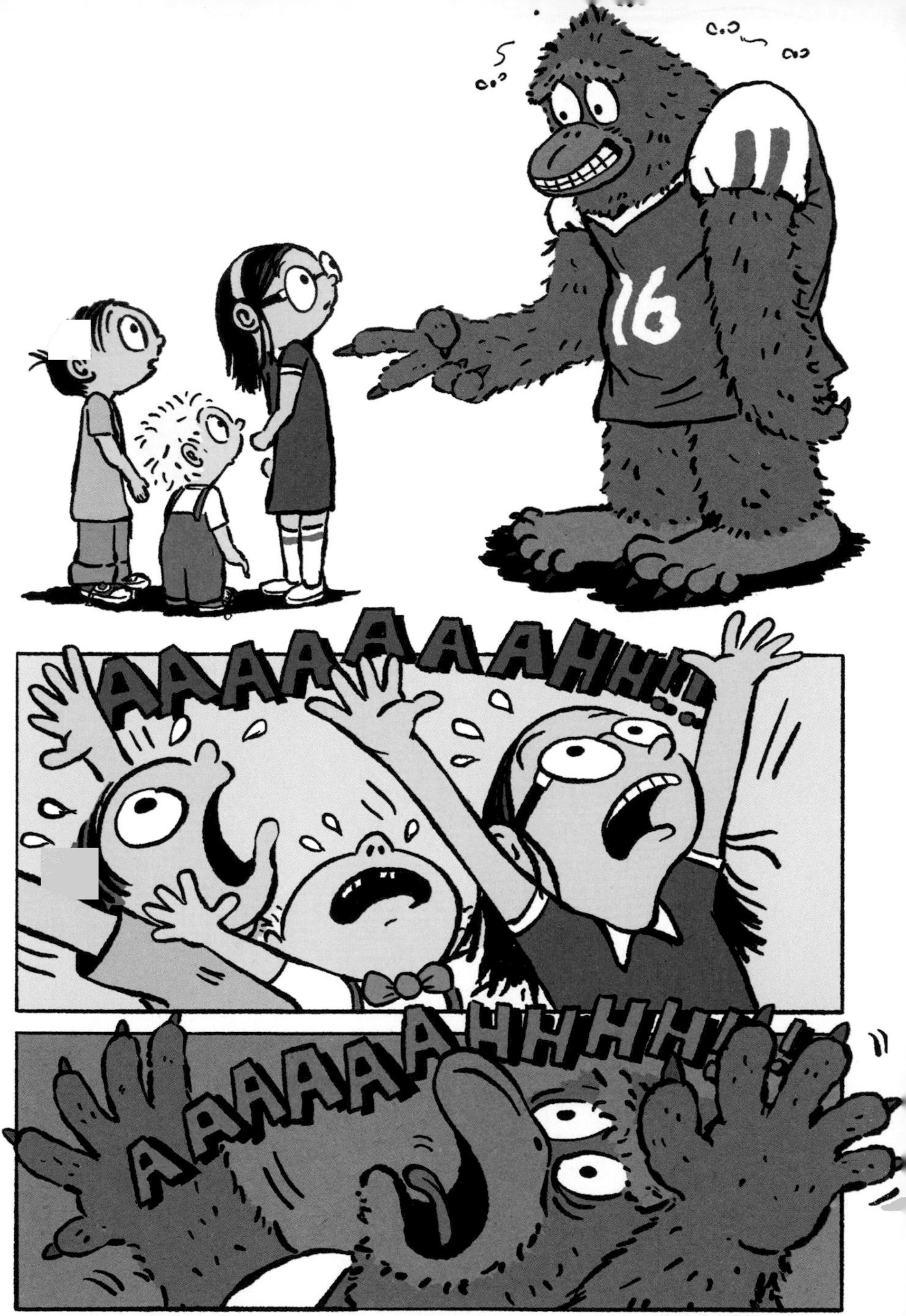
AAAAAAAHH!!...
AAAAAAHHHHH!!

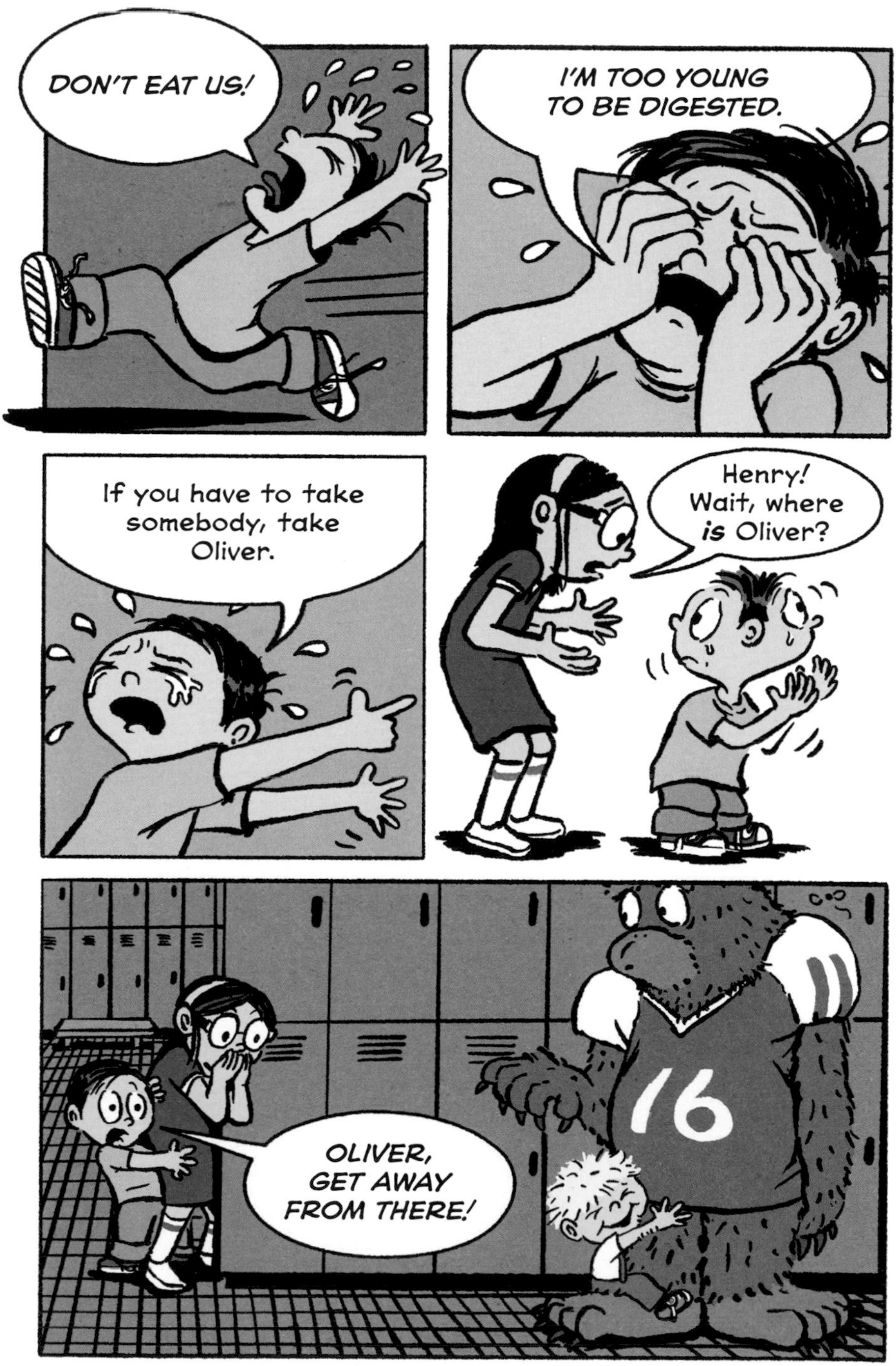
DON'T EAT US!
I'M TOO YOUNG TO BE DIGESTED.
If you have to take somebody, take Oliver.
Henry! Wait, where *is* Oliver?
OLIVER, GET AWAY FROM THERE!

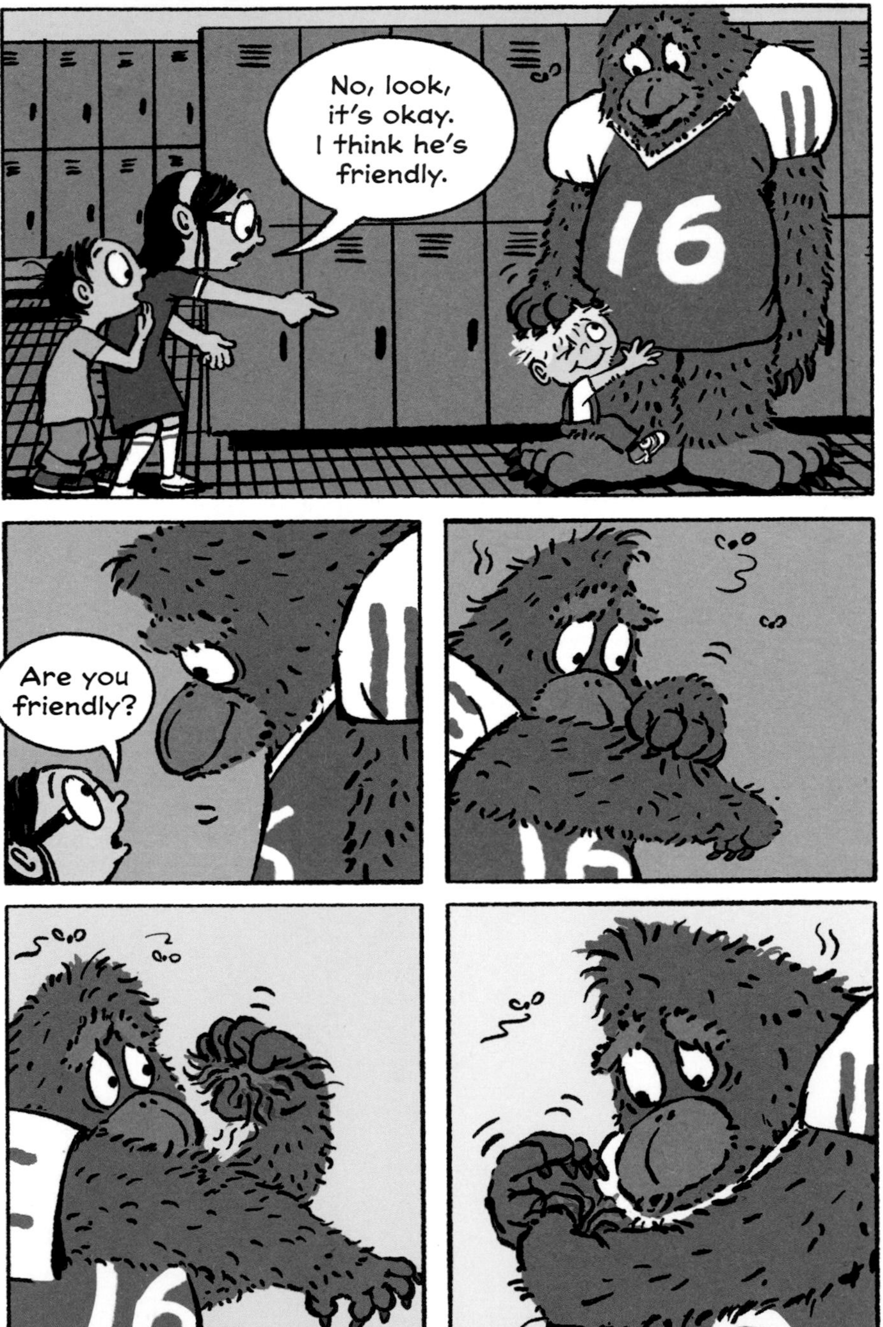
No, look, it's okay. I think he's friendly.
Are you friendly?

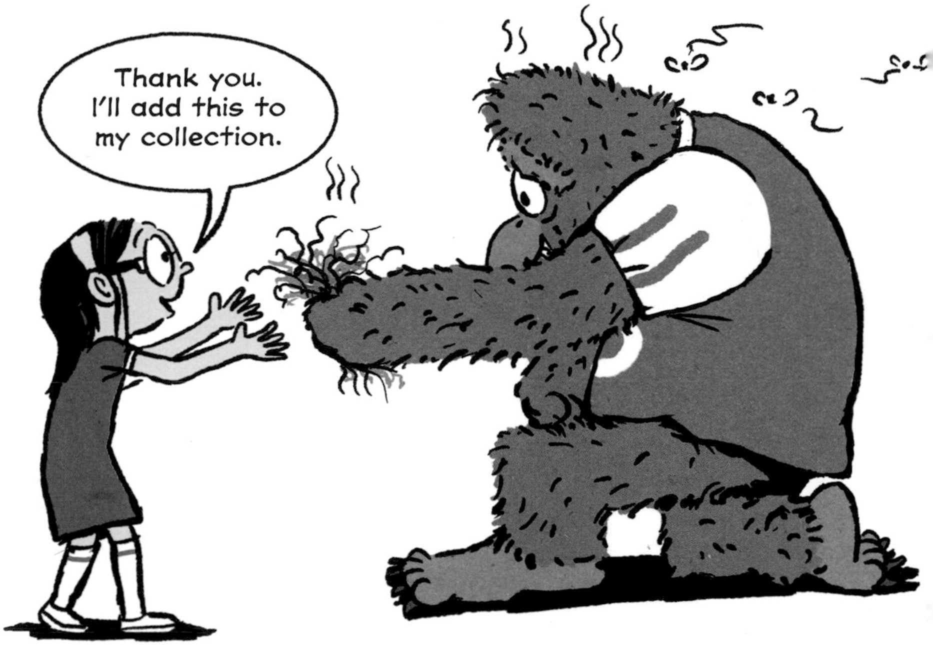
Thank you.
I'll add this to
my collection.

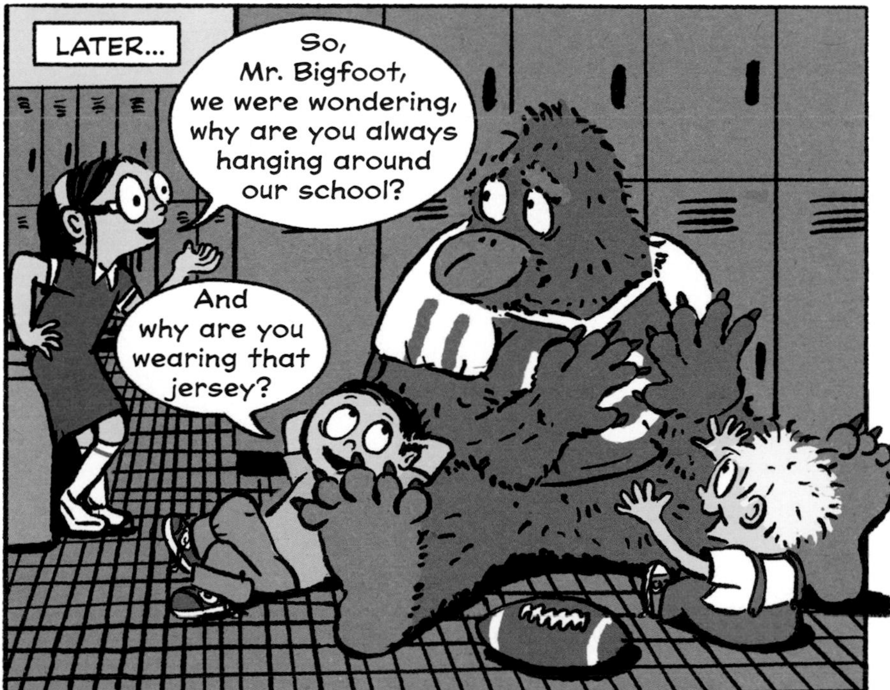
LATER...
So,
Mr. Bigfoot,
we were wondering,
why are you always
hanging around
our school?
And
why are you
wearing that
jersey?

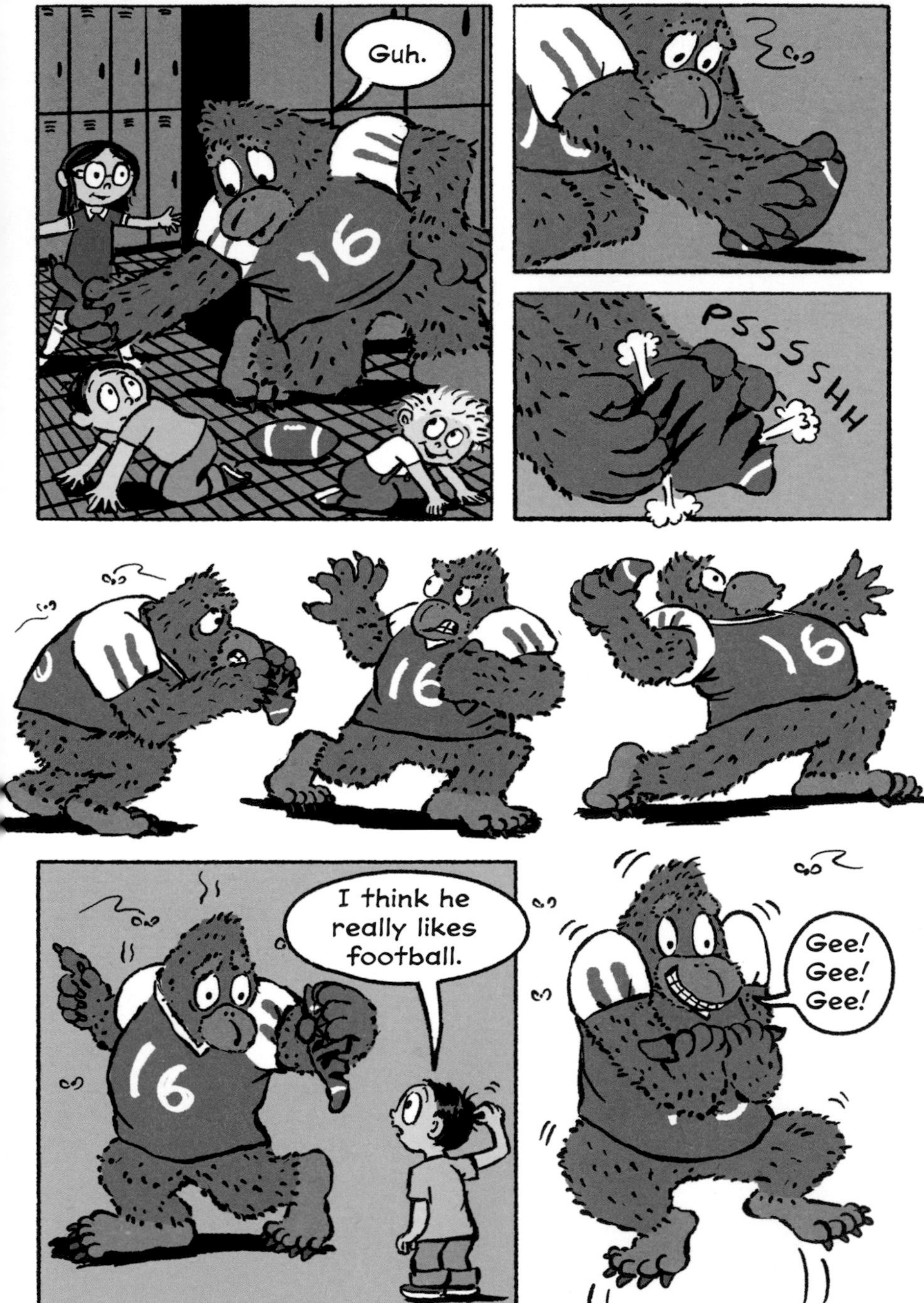
Guh.
PSSSSSHH
I think he really likes football.
Gee! Gee! Gee!

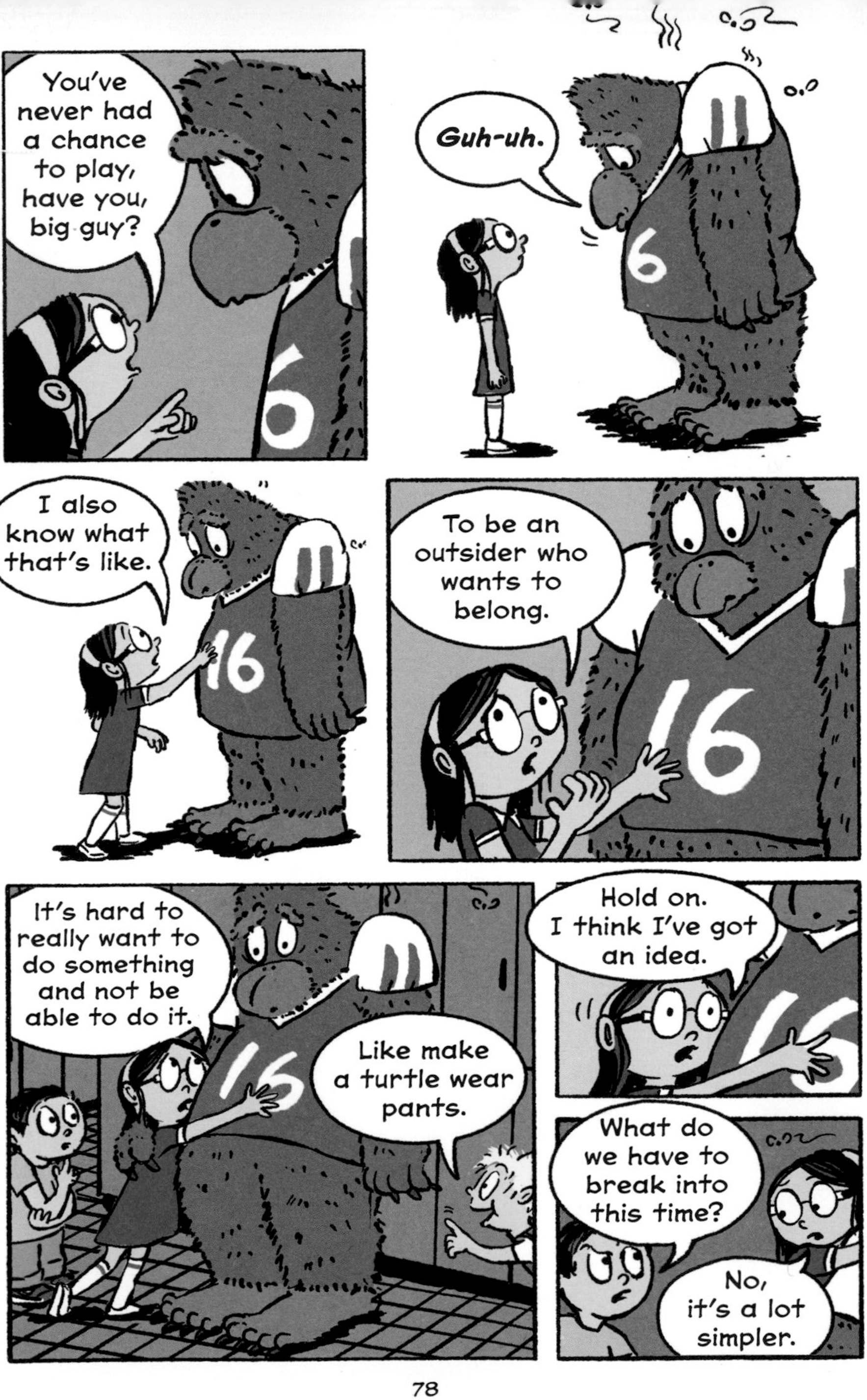
You've never had a chance to play, have you, big guy?
Guh-uh.
I also know what that's like.
To be an outsider who wants to belong.
It's hard to really want to do something and not be able to do it.
Like make a turtle wear pants.
Hold on. I think I've got an idea.
What do we have to break into this time?
No, it's a lot simpler.

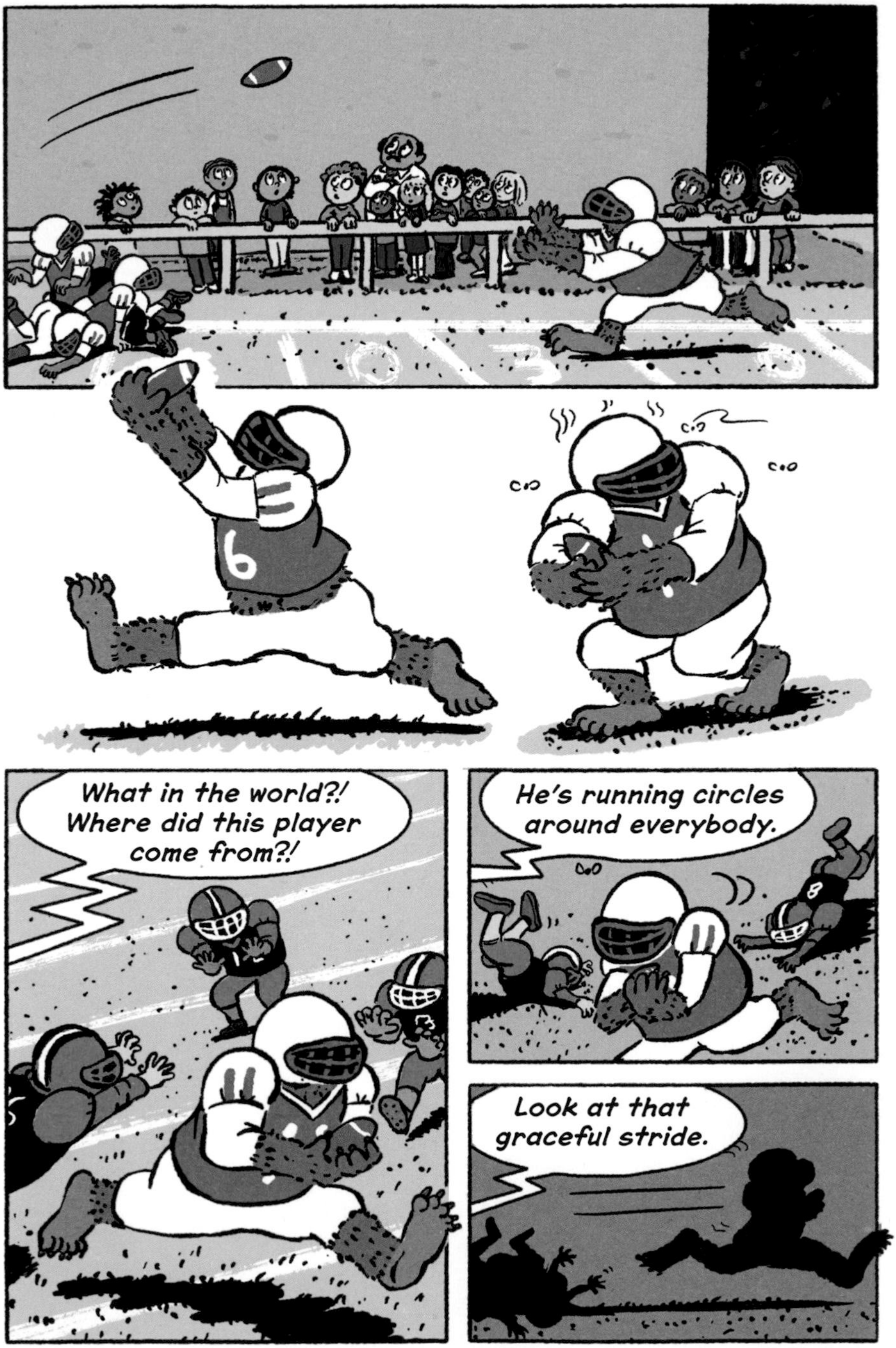
What in the world?!
Where did this player come from?!
He's running circles around everybody.
Look at that graceful stride.

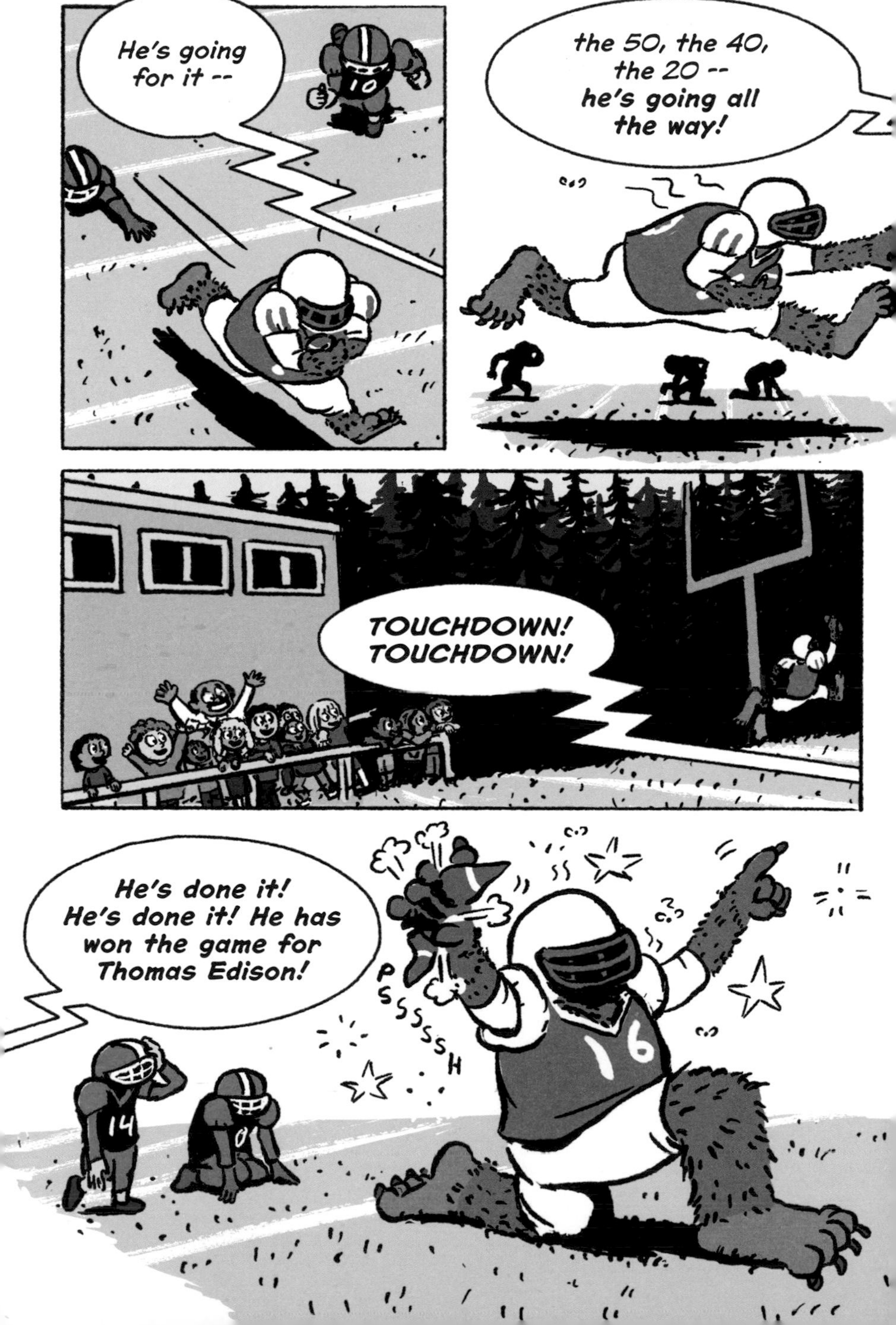

He's going for it --
the 50, the 40, the 20 -- he's going all the way!
TOUCHDOWN! TOUCHDOWN!
He's done it! He's done it! He has won the game for Thomas Edison!
PSSSSSSH

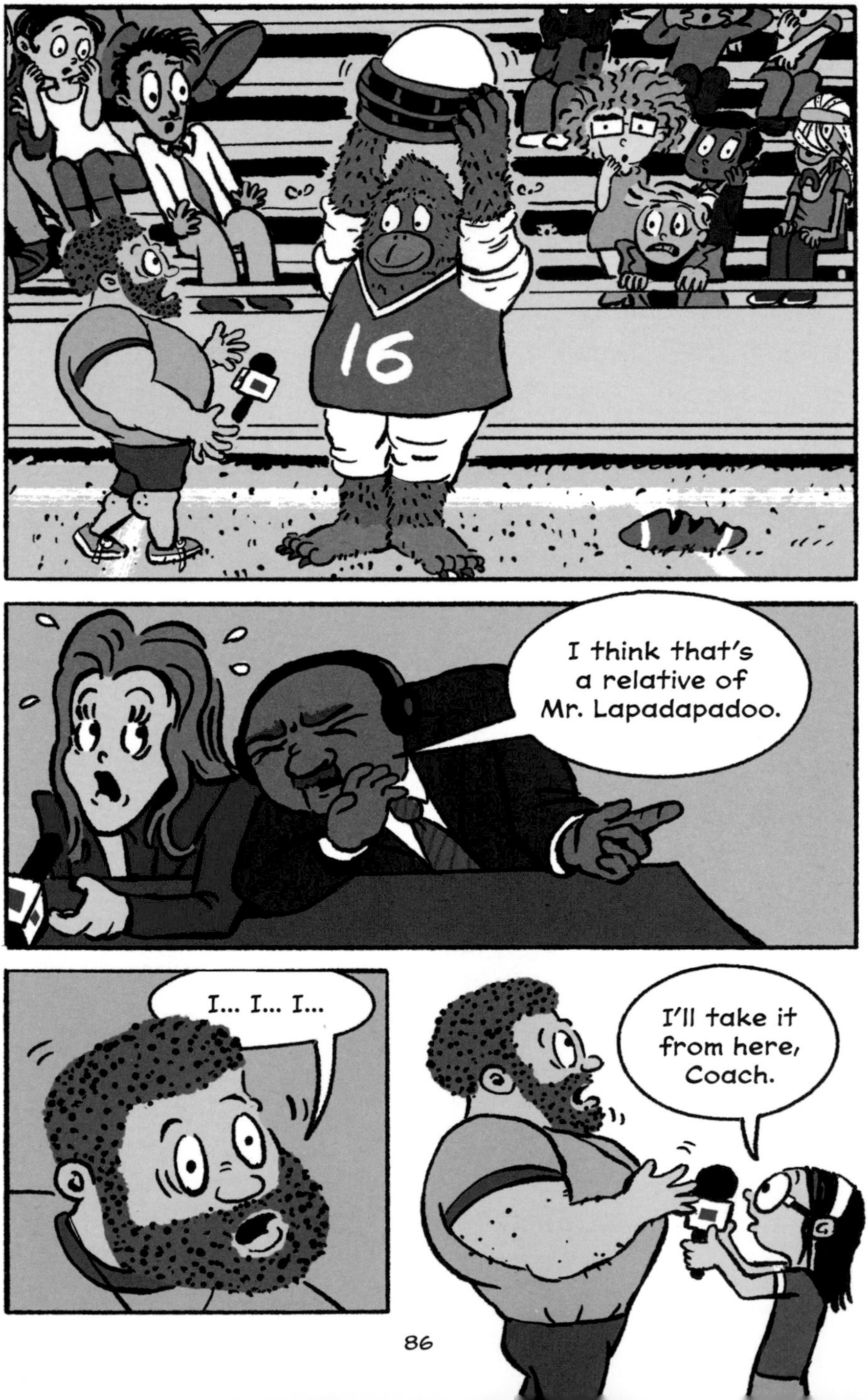
I think that's a relative of Mr. Lapadapadoo.
I... I... I...
I'll take it from here, Coach.

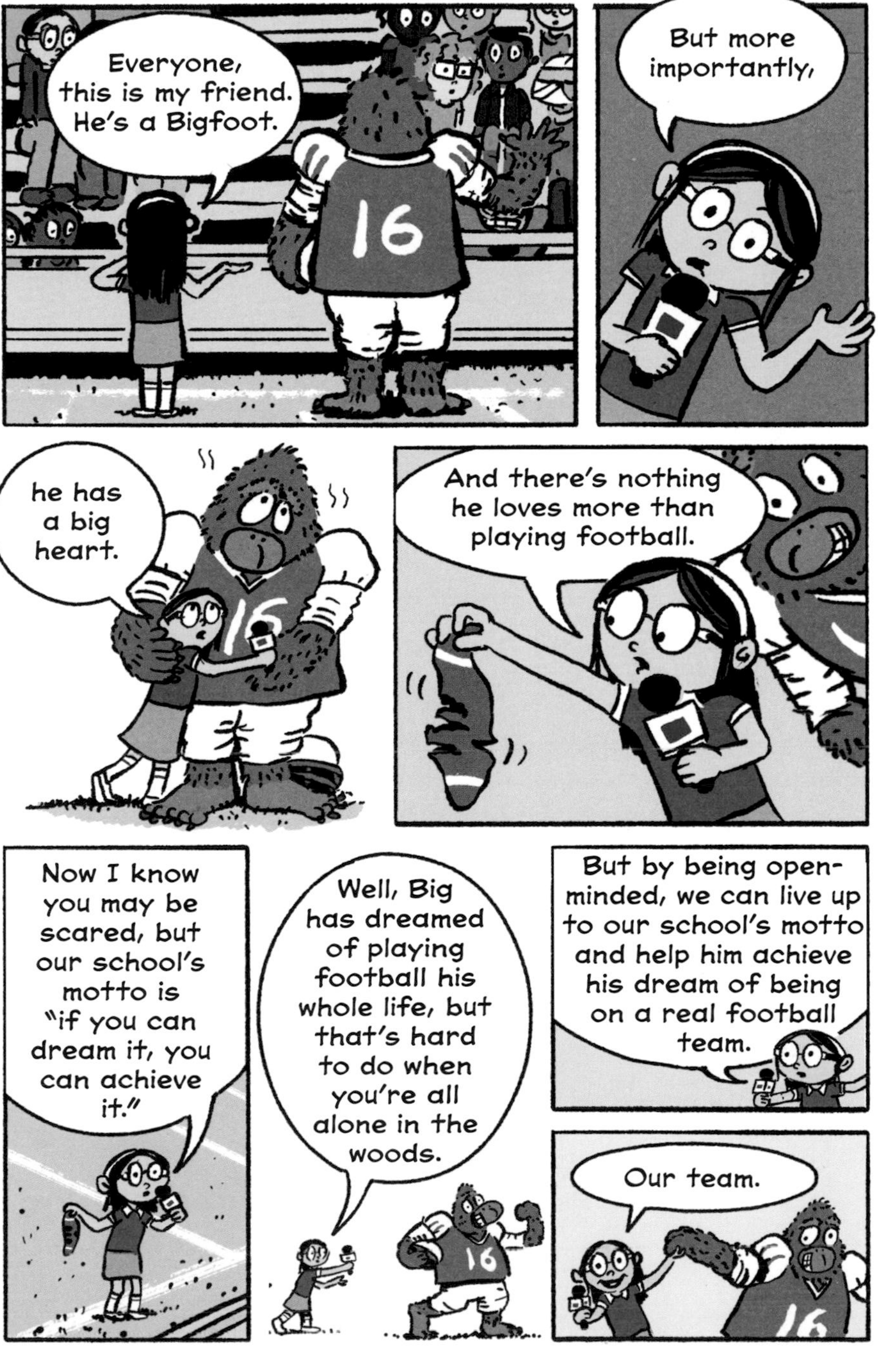
Everyone, this is my friend. He's a Bigfoot.
16
But more importantly,
he has a big heart.
16
And there's nothing he loves more than playing football.
Now I know you may be scared, but our school's motto is "if you can dream it, you can achieve it."
Well, Big has dreamed of playing football his whole life, but that's hard to do when you're all alone in the woods.
16
But by being open-minded, we can live up to our school's motto and help him achieve his dream of being on a real football team.
Our team.
16

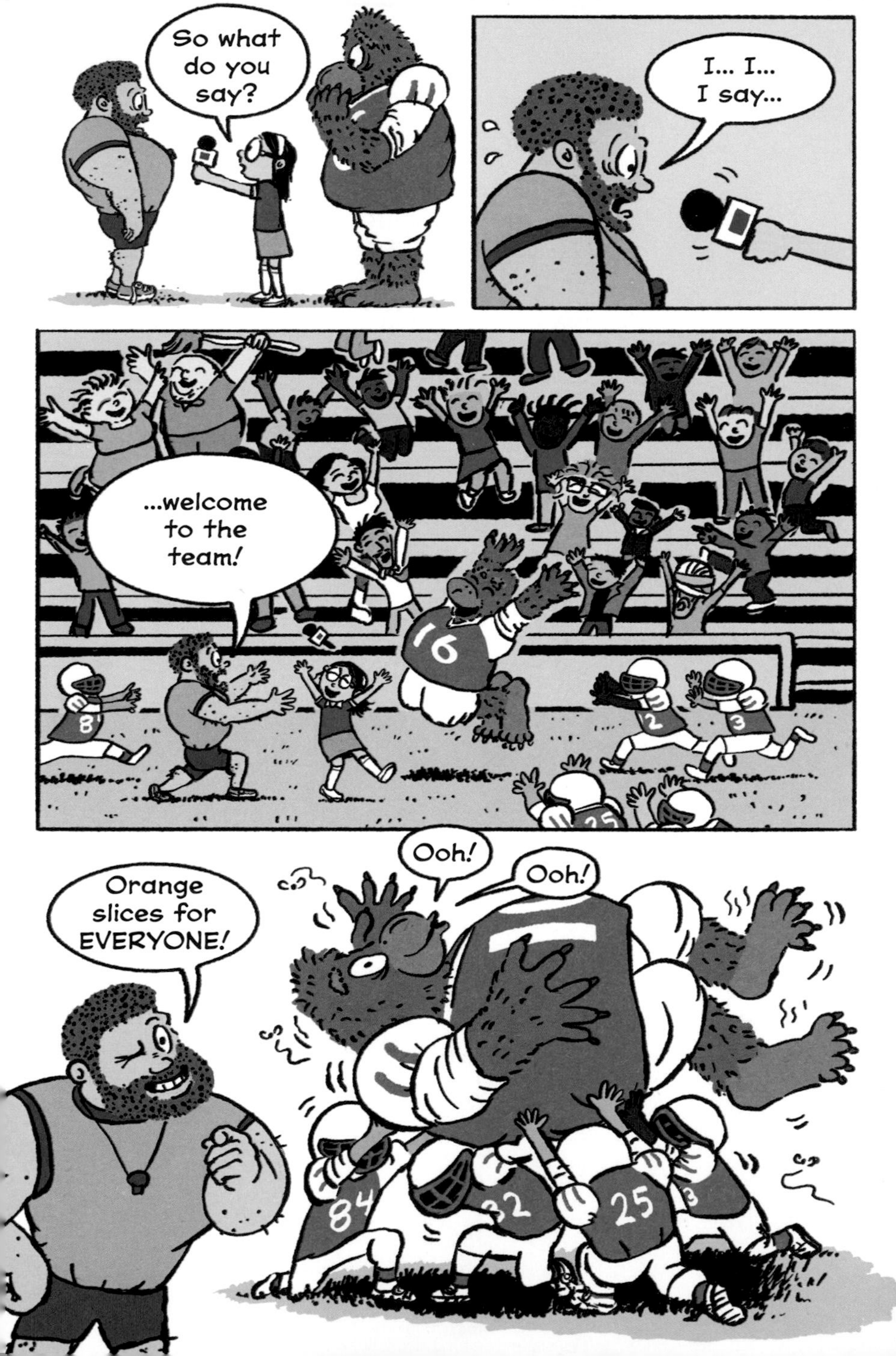
So what do you say?
I... I... I say...
...welcome to the team!
Orange slices for EVERYONE!
Ooh!
Ooh!

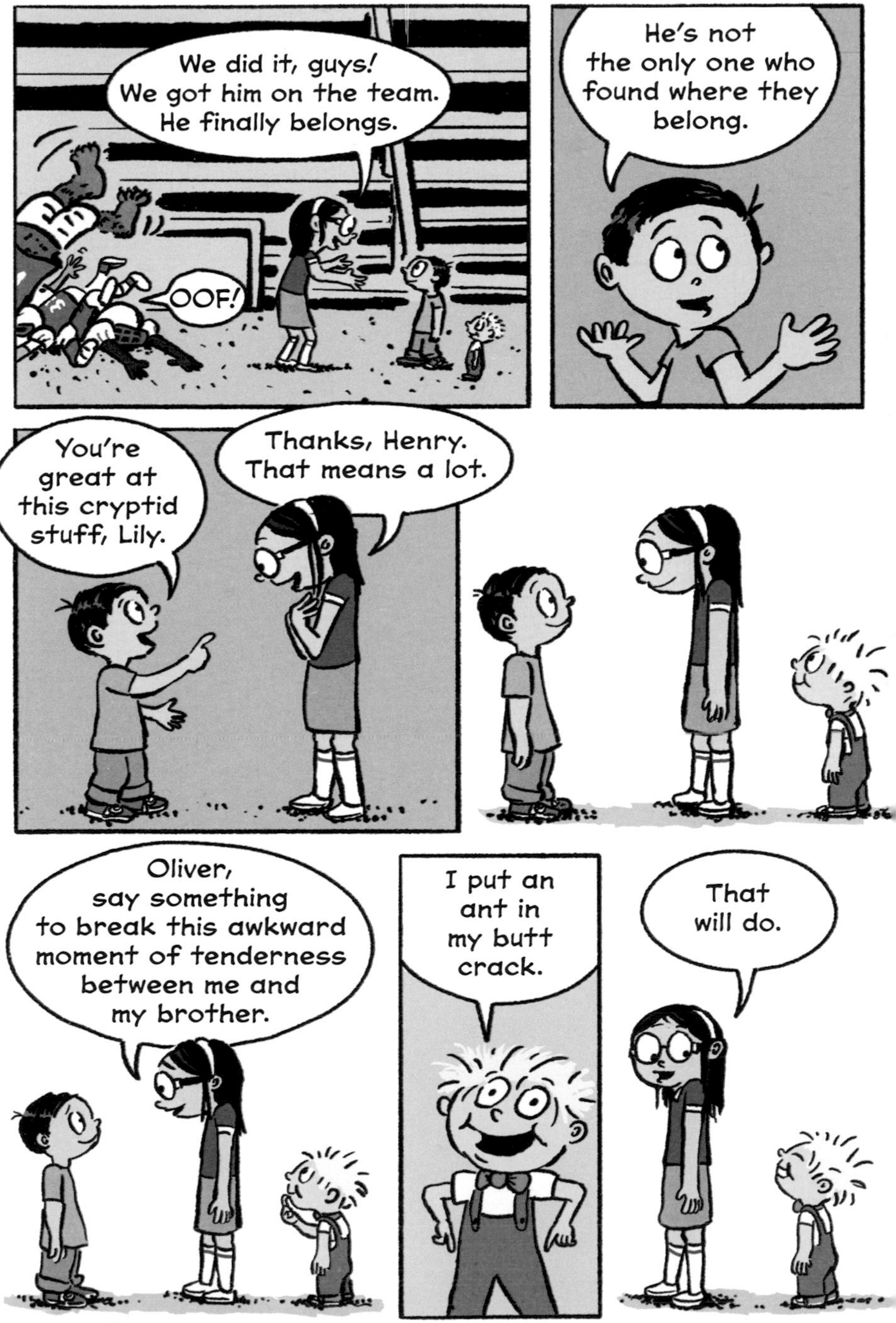
We did it, guys! We got him on the team. He finally belongs.
OOF!
He's not the only one who found where they belong.
You're great at this cryptid stuff, Lily.
Thanks, Henry. That means a lot.
Oliver, say something to break this awkward moment of tenderness between me and my brother.
I put an ant in my butt crack.
That will do.

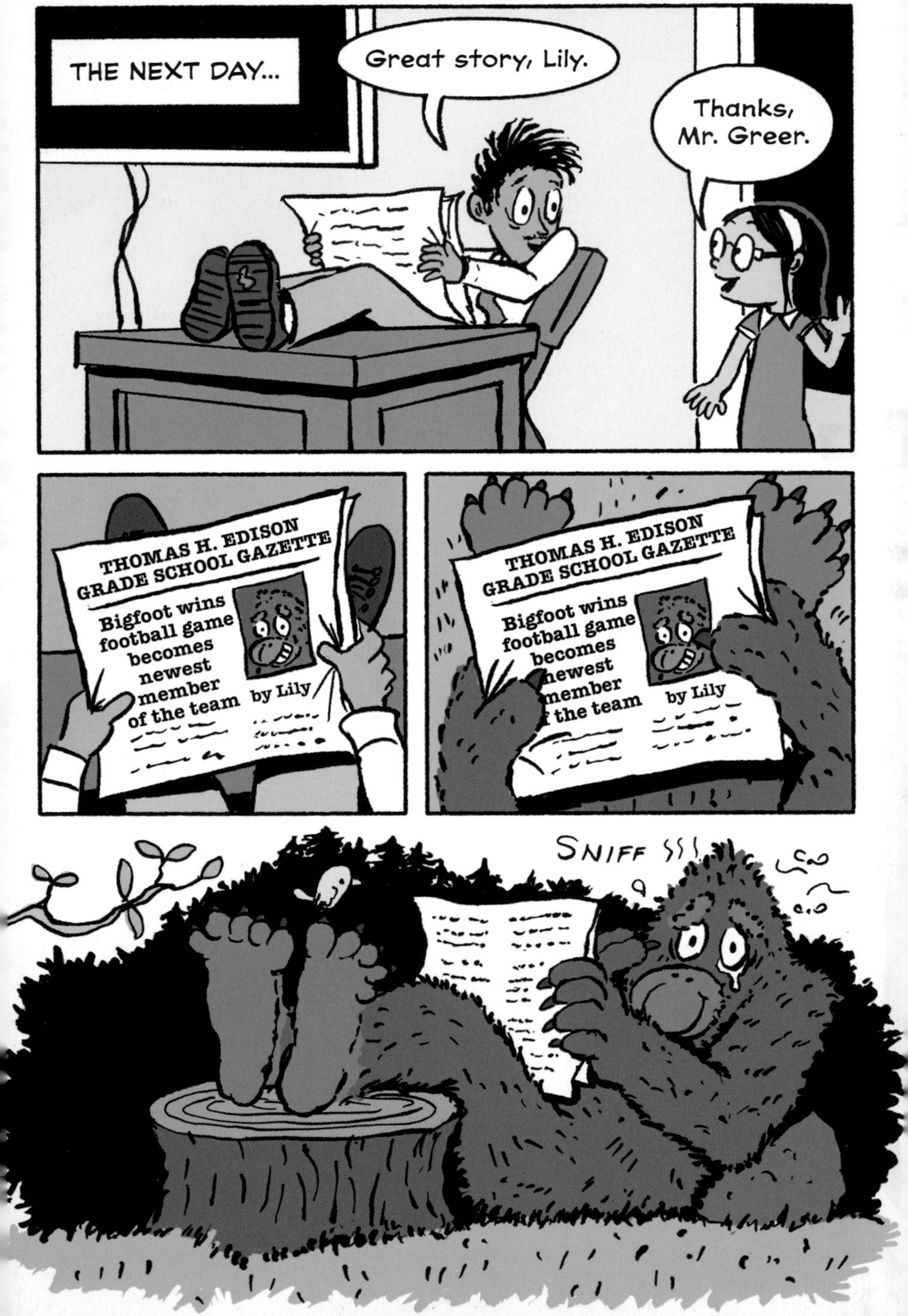
THE NEXT DAY...
Great story, Lily.
Thanks, Mr. Greer.
THOMAS H. EDISON GRADE SCHOOL GAZETTE
Bigfoot wins football game becomes newest member of the team
by Lily
THOMAS H. EDISON GRADE SCHOOL GAZETTE
Bigfoot wins football game becomes newest member of the team
by Lily
SNIFF

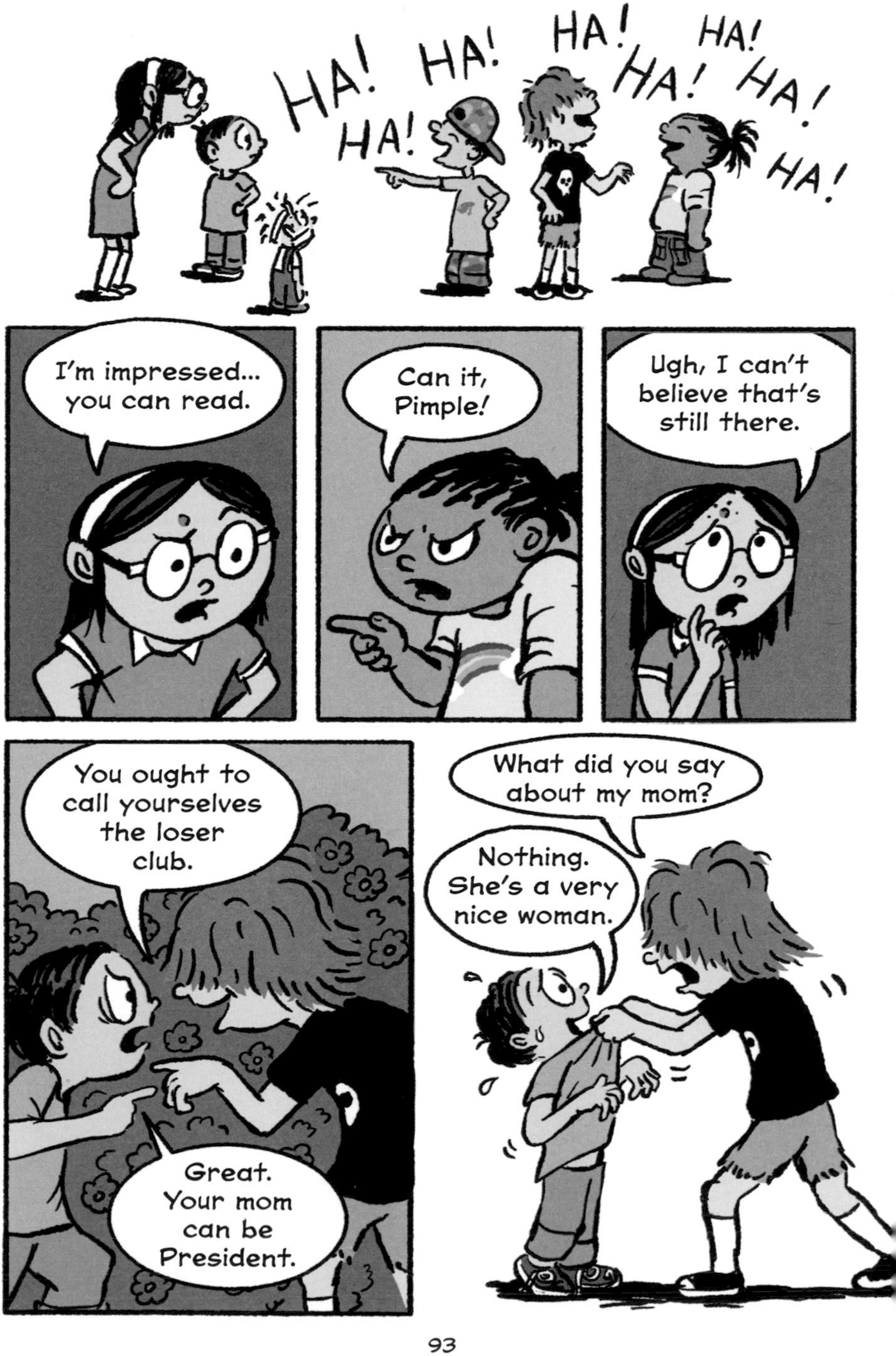
HA! HA! HA! HA! HA! HA! HA! HA!
I'm impressed... you can read.
Can it, Pimple!
Ugh, I can't believe that's still there.
You ought to call yourselves the loser club.
Great. Your mom can be President.
What did you say about my mom?
Nothing. She's a very nice woman.

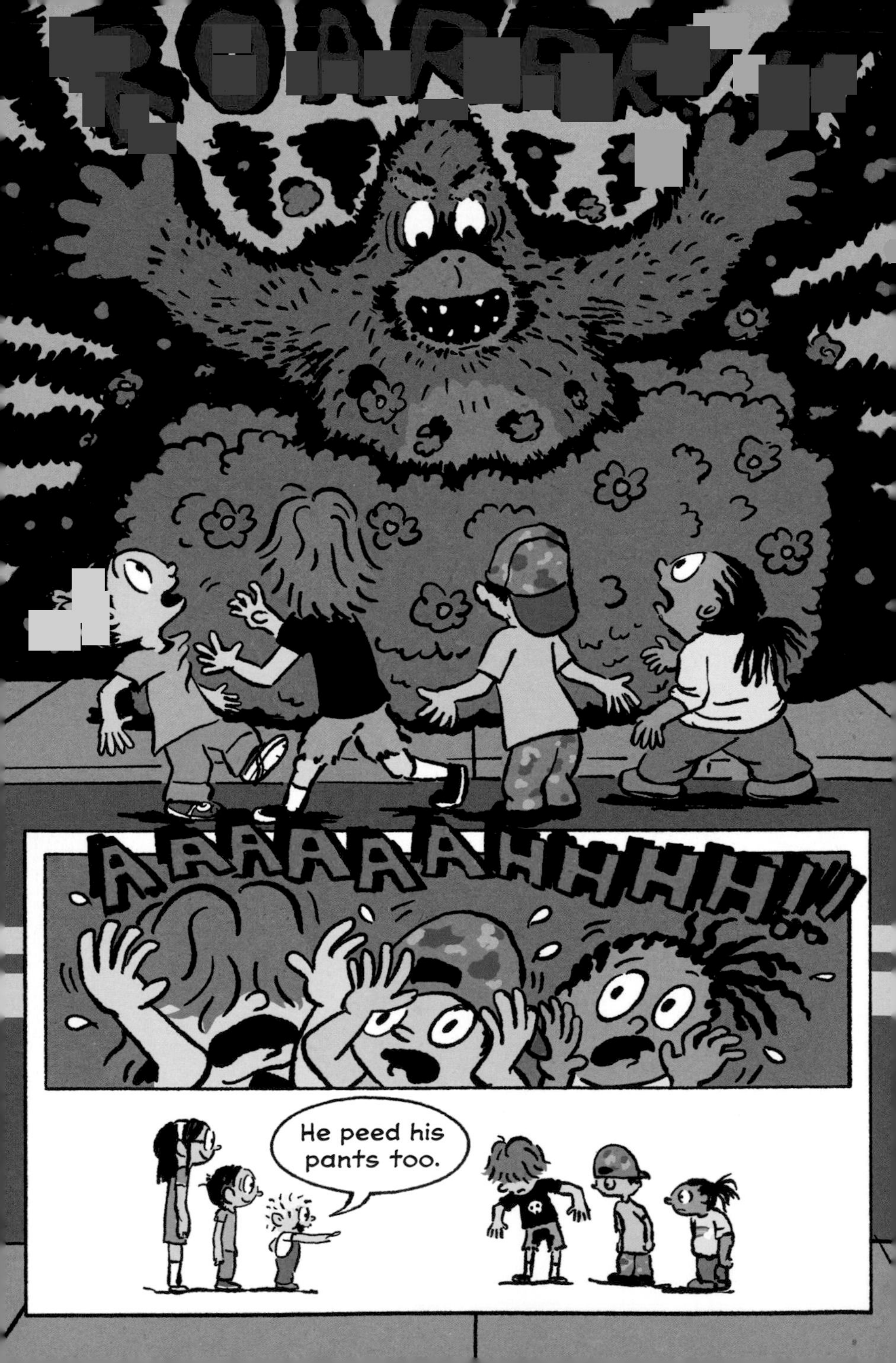
[redacted]
AAAAAAHHHHHH!!!
He peed his pants too.

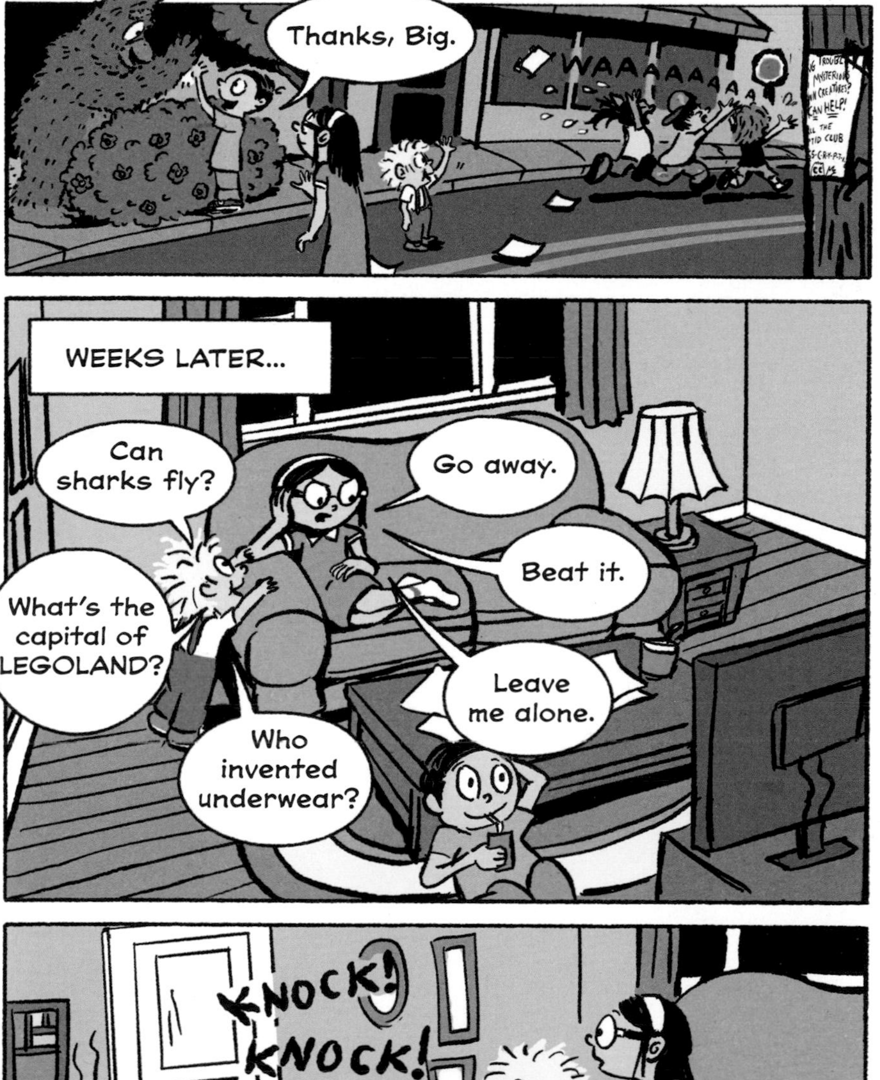
Thanks, Big.
WEEKS LATER...
Can sharks fly?
Go away.
What's the capital of LEGOLAND?
Beat it.
Who invented underwear?
Leave me alone.
KNOCK!
KNOCK!
KNOCK!

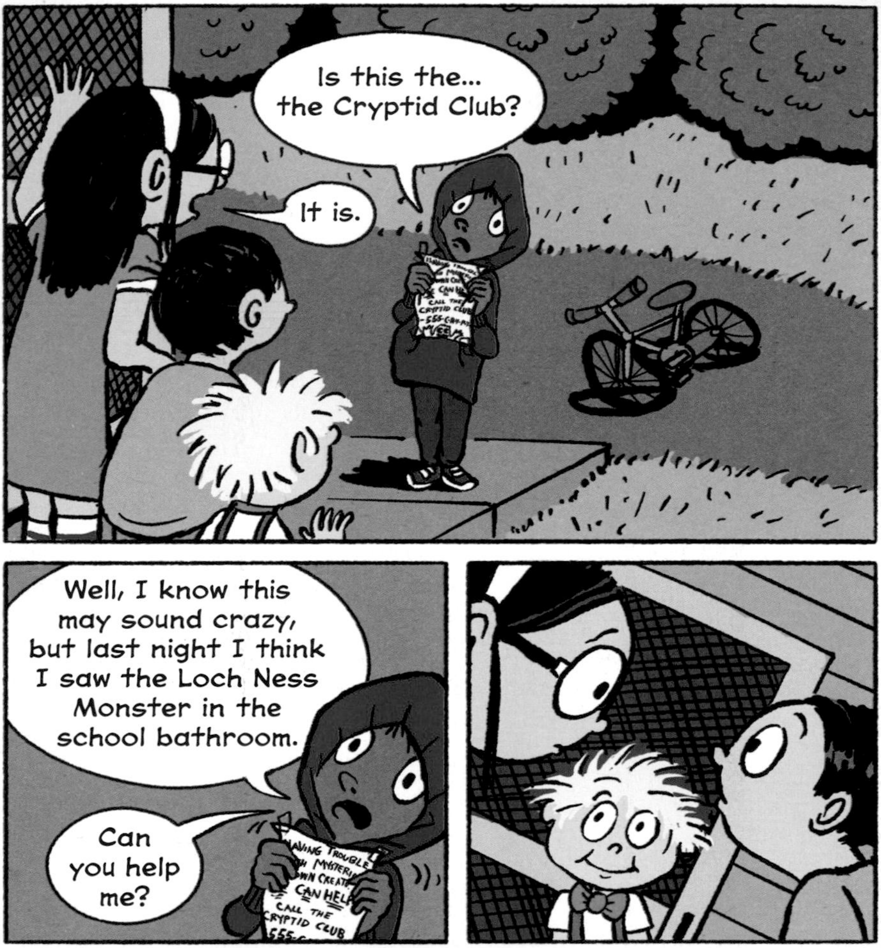
Is this the... the Cryptid Club?
It is.
Well, I know this may sound crazy, but last night I think I saw the Loch Ness Monster in the school bathroom.
Can you help me?
THE CRYPTID CLUB HQ
Yes, we can.